'An extremely fine and memorable novel'

'A fabulously benign book . . . A work of sympathetic magic'
Sebastian Barry, *Guardian*

'There unfolds a series of wrenching human dramas, which Trevor
. . . depicts with kindness and beautiful delicacy but also a kind of
implacable wisdom' Jane Shilling, *Daily Telegraph*

'Deals with dramatic and life-changing events in the calmest
and steadiest prose imaginable . . . The work of a true master'
Paul Bailey, *Independent*

'A beautiful, tender and perfectly executed story'
James Naughtie, Books of the Year, *Daily Telegraph*

'It's an extremely tense read; I felt constantly afraid. But there's a
generosity to his vision, and a surprising rightness'
David Vann, Books of the Year, *Guardian*

'The publishing event of the year . . . A beautifully told
tale of frustration and heartache'
Terry Wogan, Books of the Year, *Mail on Sunday*

'Beautifully written, as ever, elegiac and moving. No one writes about
Ireland better' Susan Hill, Books of the Year, *The Lady*

'A thrilling work of art' Thomas Mallon, *The New York Times*

'Another beautifully crafted novel . . . He belongs in a tradition
classically represented by the fiction writers of the late nineteenth
and early twentieth century like Maupassant, Chekhov and the
Joyce of *Dubliners*' David Lodge, *New York Review of Books*

'Elegiac and poignant, *Love and Summer* is a work of real beauty . . .
Essential reading' Matthew Dennison, *Country Life*

'Beautiful and entrancing, a love affair captured with
compassion and sadness' *The Times*

ABOUT THE AUTHOR

William Trevor was born in Mitchelstown, County Cork, Ireland, in 1928.
He is the author of fourteen much-lauded novels: he won the Whitbread
Prize three times and was shortlisted for the Booker Prize four times. Trevor
was widely recognized to be one of the greatest short-story writers in the
English language. In 1999 William Trevor received the prestigious David
Cohen Literature Prize in recognition of a lifetime's literary achievement,
and in 2002 he was awarded an honorary knighthood for his services to
literature. He died in 2016.

ABOUT THE COVER ARTIST

Mike McQuade is an American collage artist, whose work blurs the
boundaries between art and design.

Love and Summer

WILLIAM TREVOR

PENGUIN BOOKS

PENGUIN ESSENTIALS

UK | USA | Canada | Ireland | Australia
India | New Zealand | South Africa

Penguin Books is part of the Penguin Random House group of companies
whose addresses can be found at global.penguinrandomhouse.com.

First published by Viking 2009
Published in Penguin Books 2010
Reissued 2016
This Penguin Essentials edition published 2020

001

Copyright © William Trevor, 2009

The moral right of the author has been asserted

Printed and bound in Great Britain by Clays Ltd, Elcograf S.p.A.

A CIP catalogue record for this book is available from the British Library

ISBN: 978-0-241-98948-7

www.greenpenguin.co.uk

For Jane

On a June evening some years after the middle of the last century Mrs Eileen Connulty passed through the town of Rathmoye: from Number 4 The Square to Magennis Street, into Hurley Lane, along Irish Street, across Cloughjordan Road to the Church of the Most Holy Redeemer. Her night was spent there.

The life that had come to an end had been one of good works and resolution, with a degree of severity in domestic and family matters. The anticipation of personal contentment, which had long ago influenced Mrs Connulty's acceptance of the married state and the bearing of two children, had since failed her: she had been disappointed in her husband and in her daughter. As death approached, she had feared she would now be obliged to join her husband and prayed she would not have to. Her daughter she was glad to part from; her son – now in his fiftieth year, her pet since first he lay in her arms as an infant – Mrs Connulty had wept to leave behind.

The blinds of private houses, drawn down as the coffin went by, were released soon after it had passed. Shops that had closed opened again. Men who had uncovered their heads replaced caps or hats, children who had ceased to play in Hurley Lane were no longer constrained. The undertakers descended the steps of the church. Tomorrow's Mass would bring a bishop; until the very last, Mrs Connulty would be given her due.

People at that time said the family Mrs Connulty had married into owned half of Rathmoye, an impression created by their licensed premises in Magennis Street, their coal yards in St Matthew Street, and Number 4 The Square, a lodging house established by the Connultys in 1903. During the decades that had passed since then there had been the acquisition of other properties in the town; repaired and generally put right, they brought in modest rents that, accumulating, became a sizeable total. But even so it was an exaggeration when people said that the Connultys owned half of Rathmoye.

Compact and ordinary, it was a town in a hollow that had grown up there for no reason that anyone knew or wondered about. Farmers brought in livestock on the first Monday of every month, and borrowed money from one of Rathmoye's two banks. They had their teeth drawn by the dentist who practised in the Square, from time to time consulted a solicitor there, inspected the agricultural machinery at Des Devlin's on the Nenagh road, dealt with Heffernan the seed merchant, drank in one of the town's many public houses. Their wives shopped for groceries from the warehouse shelves of the Cash and Carry, or in McGovern's if they weren't economizing; for shoes in Tyler's; for clothes, curtain material and oilcloth in Corbally's drapery. There had once been employment at the mill, and at the mill's electricity plant before the Shannon Scheme came; there was employment now at the creamery and the condensed-milk factory, in builders' yards, in shops and public houses, at the bottled-water plant. There

2

was a courthouse in the Square, an abandoned railway station at the end of Mill Street. There were two churches and a convent, a Christian Brothers' school and a technical school. Plans for a swimming-pool were awaiting the acquisition of funds.

Nothing happened in Rathmoye, its people said, but most of them went on living there. It was the young who left – for Dublin or Cork or Limerick, for England, sometimes for America. A lot came back. That nothing happened was an exaggeration too.

The funeral Mass was on the morning of the following day, and when it was over Mrs Connulty's mourners stood about outside the cemetery gates, declaring that she would never be forgotten in the town and beyond it. The women who had toiled beside her in the Church of the Most Holy Redeemer asserted that she had been an example to them all. They recalled how no task had been too menial for her to undertake, how the hours spent polishing a surfeit of brass or scraping away old candle-grease had never been begrudged. The altar flowers had not once in sixty years gone in need of fresh water; the missionary leaflets were replaced when necessary. Small repairs had been effected on cassocks and surplices and robes. Washing the chancel tiles had been a sacred duty.

While such recollections were shared, and the life that had ended further lauded, a young man in a pale tweed suit that stood out a bit on a warm morning surreptitiously photographed the scene. He had earlier cycled the seven and a half miles from where he lived, and was then held up by the funeral traffic. He had come to photograph the town's burnt-out cinema, which he had heard about in a similar small town where recently he had photographed the perilous condition of a terrace of houses wrenched from their foundations in a landslip.

Dark-haired and thin, in his early twenties, the young man was a stranger in Rathmoye. A suggestion of stylishness – in his general demeanour, in his jaunty green-and-blue-striped tie – was repudiated by the comfortable bagginess of his suit. His features had a misleading element of seriousness in their natural cast, contributing further to this impression of contradiction. His name was Florian Kilderry.

'Whose funeral?' he enquired in the crowd, returning to it from where he had temporarily positioned himself behind a parked car in order to take his photographs. He nodded when he was told, then asked for directions to the ruined cinema. 'Thanks,' he said politely, his smile friendly. 'Thanks,' he said again, and pushed his bicycle through the throng of mourners.

Neither Mrs Connulty's son nor her daughter knew that the funeral attendance had been recorded in such a manner, and when they made their way, separately, back to Number 4 The Square they remained ignorant of this unusual development. The crowd began to disperse then, many to gather again in Number 4, others to return to their interrupted morning. The last to go was an old Protestant called Orpen Wren, who believed the coffin that had been interred contained the mortal remains of an elderly kitchenmaid whose death had occurred thirty-four years ago in a household he had known well. The respectful murmur of voices around him dwindled to nothing; cars drove off. Alone where he stood, Orpen Wren remained for a few moments longer before he, too, went on his way.

*

Cycling out of the town, Ellie wondered who the man who'd been taking photographs was. The way he'd asked about the old picture house you could tell he didn't know Rathmoye at all, and she'd never seen him on the streets or in a shop. She wondered if he was connected with the Connultys, since it was the Connultys who owned the picture house and since it had been Mrs Connulty's funeral. She'd never seen photographs taken at a funeral before, and supposed the Connultys could have employed him to do it. Or he was maybe off a newspaper, the *Nenagh News* or the *Nationalist*, because sometimes in a paper you'd see a picture of a funeral. If she'd gone back to the house afterwards she could have asked Miss Connulty, but the artificial-insemination man was expected and she'd said she'd be there.

She hurried in case she'd be late, although she had worked it out that she wouldn't be. She would have liked to go back to the house. She'd have liked to see the inside of it, which she never had, although she'd been supplying Mrs Connulty with eggs for a long time.

It could be the photographs were something the priests wanted, that maybe Father Balfe kept a parish book like she'd once been told by Sister Clare a priest might. Keeping a book would be more like Father Balfe than Father Millane, not that she knew what it would contain. She wondered if she'd be in a photograph herself. When the camera was held up to take a picture she remembered slender, fragile-seeming hands.

The white van was in the yard and Mr Brennock was getting out of it. She said she was sorry, and he said what for? She said she'd make him a cup of tea.

*

After he had spent only a few minutes at the remains of the cinema, Florian Kilderry broke his journey at a roadside public house called the Dano Mahoney. He had been interrupted at the cinema by a man who had noticed his bicycle and came in to tell him he shouldn't be there. The man had pointed out that there was a notice and Florian said he hadn't seen it, although in fact he had. 'There's permission needed,' the man crossly informed him, admitting when he snapped shut the two padlocks securing the place that they shouldn't have been left open. 'See Miss O'Keeffe in the coal yards,' he advised. 'You'll get permission if she thinks fit.' But when Florian asked about the whereabouts of the coal yards he was told they were closed today as a mark of respect. 'You'll have noticed a funeral,' the man said.

In the bar Florian took a glass of wine to a corner and lit a cigarette. He had had a wasted journey, the unexpected funeral his only compensation, and from memory he tried to recall the images of it he had gathered. The mourners had conversed in twos and threes, a priest among them, several nuns. A few, alone, had begun to move away; others had stood awkwardly, as if feeling they should stay longer. The scene had been a familiar one: he had photographed funerals before, had once or twice been asked to desist. Sometimes there was a moment of drama, or a display of uncontrollable grief, but today there had been neither.

6

On the other hand, what he had been allowed to see of the cinema was promising. Through smashed glass a poster still advertised *Idiot's Delight*, the features of Norma Shearer cut about and distorted. He'd been scrutinizing them when the man shouted at him, but he never minded something like that. The Coliseum the cinema had been called, Western Electric sound newly installed.

A smell of frying bacon wafted into the bar, and voices on a radio. Sporting heroes – wrestlers, boxers, jockeys, hurlers – decorated the walls, with greyhounds and steeple-chasers. The publican, a framed newspaper item declared, had been a pugilist himself, had gone five rounds with Jack Doyle, the gloves he'd worn hanging from a shelf behind the bar. 'Give a rap on the old counter if you'd want a refill,' he advised when a woman summoned him to the meal she'd cooked. But Florian said the single glass would be enough. He sat for a while longer, finishing a second cigarette, and then carried his empty glass to the bar. A voice called out goodbye and invited him to look in again. He said he would.

Outside, in warm afternoon sunshine, he stood for a few minutes, eyes half closed, his back against one of the entrance-door pillars. Then, riding slowly, he continued his journey. He lived alone. He wasn't in a hurry.

*

The day advanced in Rathmoye. Disturbed by death, the town settled again into its many routines. Number 4 The Square was put to rights after nearly a hundred sympathizers had accepted the invitation to funeral refreshment. Trays of cups and saucers were carried down from the vast first-floor sitting-room to the kitchen, scattered glasses gathered up, windows thrown open, ashtrays emptied. By the time the stairs had been hoovered, tea-towels hung up to dry and the daily girl sent home, it was evening.

Alone in the house, as she had not been since the death, Mrs Connulty's daughter fondled the jewellery that now was hers: strings of lapis and jade, garnet and amber, the sapphire earrings, the turquoise, the pearls, the opals, the half-hoops of diamonds, the ruby engagement ring, the three cameos. There was a rosary too, but it did not properly belong, being of little value compared with the finery.

In her middle age, Miss Connulty was known in Rathmoye no more intimately than that – a formality imposed upon her when, twenty years ago, her mother ceased to address her by either of the saints' names she had been given at her birth. Unconsciously, her brother had followed this example, and when her father died she was nameless in the house. By now, 'Miss Connulty' belonged to her more naturally in the town than the form of address she had once enjoyed there.

Thirty-two pieces she counted, not one of them unfamiliar to her, and she would wear them and wear them often, as her mother had. This reflection came coolly, without emotion. Some of the pieces would suit her, some would not. 'What are you doing, child?' her mother had long ago sharply demanded, unexpectedly in this same room, her slippered feet making no sound. A garnet necklace draped her child's neck, not hooked at the back, the clasp held between finger and thumb. It dropped with a clatter on to the dressing-table, and Mrs Connulty, tall and stoutly made, declared that the Guards must be sent for.

'Don't get the Guards! Oh, don't, don't!' Her own cry of alarm came back to Miss Connulty from childhood, fear cold again in her stomach. 'Go out for a Guard, Kitty,' her mother called down the stairs to a startled maid, and ordered the necklace to be put away. She went through the pieces to see that they were all there. A Guard was in the hall then, and her mother ordered her to tell him, and when she did he shook his head at her.

Less tall than her mother, and not stout at all, Miss Connulty retained the shadow of a prettiness that had enlivened her as a girl. Grey streaked her hair, darkening its fairness, but few lines aged her features. Even so, she often felt old, and resented this reminder that in reaching middle age and passing through most of it she had missed too much of what she might have had. She returned the jewellery to the top drawer of the dressing-table that had been her mother's and now was hers. She kept out only the garnet necklace, admiring it against the drab shade of her mourning.

*

Joseph Paul Connulty was a lanky, weasel-faced man with grey hair brushed straight back and gleaming beneath a regular application of Brylcreme. Spectacles dangled on a tape around his neck, falling on to the dark serge of his suit. Two ballpoint pens were clipped into his outside breast pocket. The emblem of the Pioneer movement was prominent on his left lapel.

At a loss after he had been to the cemetery again in

order to linger on his own by the closed grave, he went to the coal yards. The sheds were locked, there was a notice on the office door; sacks that bore his name were stacked upright on a lorry, waiting to be delivered. He felt at home here, had all his life known the mounds of slack, the stables where once there'd been horses, the high gates sheeted with corrugated iron, its red paint worn away in places. In childhood he had played here, but had not been allowed in the public house, which even now – teetotaller that he was – felt alien to him, although he spent most of every day there. His hope had been to become a priest, but the vocation had slipped away from him, lost beneath the weight of his mother's doubt that he would make a success of the religious life. In the end her doubt became his own.

He locked the high gates behind him when he left and did not hurry on his way to Number 4 The Square. He passed the public house, closed also, and the deadness of the place gave him pleasure, for usually music and a muddle of voices spilt out on to the street. It was quiet, too, in the hall of the house where, being a bachelor, he took his meals and slept, where all his life he had lived.

'A garden of remembrance has been mentioned to me,' he passed on to his sister when they met on the first-floor landing.

Although they were more than brother and sister, having been born in the same few minutes, they had never shared a resemblance. In childhood they had been close companions but often now did not communicate with one another for weeks on end, though less through not being on speaking terms than having nothing to say.

'Her standing in the town,' Joseph Paul went on, answering his sister's question about the necessity for a garden of remembrance. 'Her association with the church. The money she gave, as well as everything.'

He didn't reveal the other suggestions as to a suitable memorial that had been put to him on his walk through the town, since none of them would have been more acceptable to his sister, and he was in favour of a garden himself. 'How she was,' he said instead.

Unlike the coal yards and the public house, Number 4 The Square had undergone a transition that reflected the mores of its two generations as a business place. Originally catering for permanent residents, offering three meals a day, it had become a bed-and-breakfast stop-over for commercial travellers. The present Connultys could remember, though faintly, the bank clerks and shopmen who returned each midday to the dining-room and in the evenings shared the same daily newspaper and sat around the same coal fire. McNamara the road surveyor, Superintendent Fee, Miss Neely the lay teacher at the convent, and others in their time had remained as residents until marriage or professional advancement brought a change in their lives. Each had been allocated a distinctive napkin ring; Miss Neely had her iron pills, McNamara his stout, for which there was a charge. Now only Gohery the metalwork instructor – at present away on his summer holidays – was a permanent lodger at Number 4; but the house's reputation for food and cleanliness saw to it that a room was rarely vacant. A sign in one of the ground-floor windows set out the overnight terms, and the value offered guaranteed brisk business no matter what the season.

In all this, Joseph Paul foresaw little change, the only one being that his sister would run things on her own. A woman or a girl had always come in to clean and wash up, and could not be dispensed with. Nor would his sister wish to do so.

'It's only it was raised with me,' he said. 'A garden.'

They had played a game with pieces of coal in the yards, five pieces each, to be kicked around the course they set out: to the sack shed and then to the water barrels, to the slack mounds, over the cobbles to where the carts were, beyond them to the pump and the red half-door, back to the beginning. In the town they had knocked on hall doors and run away. They had opened henhouse latches, releasing hens to chase. They had roamed the streets, their father indulgent, their mother occupied with the running of the house. Minutes younger, Joseph Paul had also been the smaller, but he had never considered that a deprivation.

'What about the gravestone?' Miss Connulty picked up a used match, overlooked by the daily girl on one of the landing windowsills. He watched her dropping it into the unlit fire in the big front room, cleverly positioning it so that it wouldn't show. He said: 'We'll go to Hegarty for that.'

'There'll be talk about the way she wants it done.'

Their mother had laid it down that she did not wish to have her name added to her husband's gravestone, preferring to have a grave and gravestone to herself.

'Her own grave's her due,' Joseph Paul said.

'Who mentioned a garden?'

'Madge Shea in Feeney's.'

A garden was what there'd never been at Number 4,

and it was this that people remembered their mother often saying. A place for meditation, Joseph Paul went on, a way of giving thanks for a life: that was what people were thinking of too, now that this time had come. Behind the church, between the church and the cemetery, there was space enough for a garden.

'It's enough we have the peculiarity of the grave,' his sister countered. 'It's the normal thing for a woman to go to rest beside her husband. It's the normal thing for a husband and a wife to share a tombstone.'

He didn't deny that, he didn't argue. The arrangement about the burial had been agreed with Father Millane and carried out as the last wishes of the dead. In the same way, Hegarty in the stoneyard would be instructed when the moment came. There would be a garden of remembrance because the people of the town wanted it.

'I heard it there was a man photographing the funeral,' his sister said.

'I didn't see that.'

'It was remarked upon in the house here. It was wondered did we want photographs.'

'I didn't see any man.'

'I'm only telling you what was said.'

She went away without further comment, taking with her a cup and saucer that had been overlooked behind a vase. Joseph Paul passed into the big front room, where the evening lamps had been lit all day, the blinds drawn on two tall windows at each of which tasselled stays were looped around velvet curtains in a shade of russet. A profusion of net provided daytime privacy. Magazines were laid out on tables and on a stool in front of the fireplace.

Ornamental elephants and their young strode the white amber-veined marble of the mantelpiece, above which Daniel O'Connell was framed in ebony.

He had been told about photographs being taken because it would worry him to hear it, because there was a lack of respect, a funeral photographed like a carnival would be. He wondered if she'd made it up; she often made things up.

He leafed through the *Nationalist*, left behind by one of last week's overnight lodgers. Then, equally without interest, he turned the pages of an old *Dublin Opinion*. She wasn't easy. He had watched her becoming devious over the years, and had hoped – had on a few occasions begged in prayer – that time would ease her discontent. When they were children their mother had liked to have her in the kitchen and often he was sent away to play by himself. He had looked through the crack when the kitchen door wasn't quite closed, as mostly it wasn't. He had watched her being shown how to tease out fat and sinew and which way to cut the meat, how to dust the pieces with flour, never too thickly. Their mother had instructed her in how long the simmering should be, when to add the dumplings, the Bisto. The day came when she was allowed to make a dumpling herself, another day when she might skin the apples for a pie, another when she might stir the custard and mash potatoes. The kitchen was their place, they were the women of the house – they and whichever maid it was, a girl from the country, or a widow of the town who needed the money.

Becoming used to this woman's world, Joseph Paul hadn't minded in the end. He chopped kindling in the outhouse, which their mother said was more a boy's thing. She took him shopping with her sometimes, she called him her little fellow. He couldn't make her cross, she said; he hadn't it in him to make her cross. Every morning after breakfast they had sat together at the fire, not a yard from where he sat now.

He had the room to himself this evening because the notice that offered accommodation had been temporarily taken down. He listened to sounds that were familiar coming from the floor below: his sister bolting the front door, a rattle of cutlery in the dining-room, the sideboard drawer being pushed in, the windows that had been opened for airing closed and latched. There had always been the chance that she would marry, that the past she had never recovered from would at last be forgotten, that Gohery, or Hickey from the watch shop, would show an interest, that one of the men who came regularly for a night would, or one of the older bachelors in the town. She had been young when the trouble happened. She hadn't let herself go when it was over. She hadn't since.

He heard her footstep, light on the stairs, the footstep he knew best now that their mother's would not be heard again. That he should be despised by his sister was one of blaming's variations; he was aware of that and it made it easier that he was. She crossed the landing and came to stand near where he sat. The two back bedrooms should be decorated before the winter, she said, the same paint as before.

He nodded. Not looking round, not wanting to see the jewellery she wore to provoke him, he said he'd attend to the matter and she went away.

2

Dillahan rose before his wife. Downstairs, he pulled out the dampers of the Rayburn stove and listened for the flutter of flames beginning before he tipped in anthracite. He waited for the kettle to boil, then made tea and shaved himself at the sink. In the yard, when he had opened the back door, his two sheepdogs ambled out of the shed where they slept to greet him. He murmured to them softly, one finger of each hand idly caressing their heads. He could tell from the air that it wasn't going to rain today.

The dogs fell in behind him when he crossed the yard, unaffected – as he was not – when they passed the bad place. A sheepdog of that time used to make a detour, hardly noticeable, but Dillahan always knew what that dog was uneasy about. On the track to the river-field a rabbit took fright, darting into the undergrowth, and then another did. In the field the ewes were undisturbed.

Dillahan counted them, seventy-four, all of them there. He watched them for a while, leaning on the iron gate, the sheepdogs crouched at his feet. Then he passed on, climbing up to the hill pasture. He called the few cows he kept for milking and they came slowly to him.

*

Ellie pulled back the bedclothes on her husband's side of the bed, then on hers. When she had washed in the farmhouse's small bathroom she drew on her nightdress again in order to cross the landing, even though she knew she was alone in the house. She dressed, combed and brushed her hair, bothering with no more than that so early in the day.

Younger by several years than her burly husband, she had something of the demeanour of a child. Yet while childhood still influenced this expression of her nature it was a modest beauty that otherwise, and more noticeably, distinguished her now. It was there in the greyish blue of eyes that had once been anxious, in the composed smile that had once been faltering and uncertain. Soft fair hair, once difficult, was now drawn back, the style that suited it best. But in the farmhouse, and the yard and the dairy, in the crab-apple orchard and the fields, though touched by the grace that time had brought, Ellie Dillahan remained as diffident a presence as she'd been when first she came here as a general maid.

This morning, as every morning in the kitchen, the dripping she had cut from the bowl softened in the frying-pan while she laid out knives and forks on the table. It was another twenty minutes before she heard her husband in the yard, before the latch of the kitchen door was lifted and he brought the milk in. He said the buzzard hawk was circling again. He took his wellington boots off at the door.

'I'll be down in the river-field a while.' He broke a silence to say that when they had finished breakfast. He had made sandwiches to take with him, which he did whenever he was likely to be in the fields all day. Making them for himself was something he had become used to during his years as a widower – cheese, tomato, anything there was. Ellie had filled his flask.

'Thanks,' he said, picking it up when she was clearing the dishes from the table.

She carried them to the sink, ran in hot water and left them to soak while she moved the chairs out from the table to make sweeping the floor's uneven surface easier. She prodded a brush as far under the dresser as it would go, reaching for whatever dust had accumulated since yesterday. She added what she'd gathered to the pile she'd made in front of the stove and then scooped everything up in the dustpan. Although her back was to her husband, she knew he was standing by the door, as if about to say something, as if that was why he hesitated there. But all he said was:

'It'll take me the day.'

'Will I bring down a drink?'

'Do, later on.'

'I will of course.' She opened the top of the stove and emptied the dustpan on to the coals.

'Take care with that,' he said.

'I forgot.' She was cross with herself. It wasn't that she had forgotten he'd told her not to be always opening the top of the Rayburn, but that she'd thought he wasn't still in the kitchen. His movements were always quiet: she had thought he was going when he said to bring the drink later.

'I'm sorry,' she said, turning to face him.

'Arrah, it doesn't matter. Take money from the book if the insurance fellow comes. I don't know has he settled on a day yet?'

'The second Thursday it was with Mr Cauley.'

'It was.' It would be different now, he said, a new man would have his own day. 'If he calls in today he'll say what it is.'

'I'll ask him if he doesn't say.'

'You'd miss old Cauley.'

The door to the yard closed behind him. She heard the tractor started, and listened to the sound fading as he drove it away. He was good to her, not minding when she made mistakes, not saying when she didn't come up to scratch, still learning the ways of the farmhouse. She told herself that, dropping the iron disc into place on the stove. She hung up the dustpan, and the sweeping brush next to it, in the cupboard under the stairs. She opened the two windows as she did every morning, even when it was raining, to let the air in for a while. She settled the sash props into position and turned back the clock on the dresser, correcting the twelve minutes it had gained since yesterday. Standing on a chair, she took a five-pound note for the insurance man from the pages of an out-of-date *Old Moore's Almanac* on the top shelf of the dresser, so that she wouldn't have to do it in front of him if he came.

The kitchen wasn't large, dominated by the width and length of this big green dresser and the oak table at which all meals were taken. The ceiling was beamed, dark timbers with whitewash between them. All the other woodwork – of the doors and window-frames and skirting-boards – was green to match the dresser. When Ellie had come to this kitchen five years ago she hadn't known a kitchen she liked as much, or known the comfort of the sitting-room at the front of the farmhouse, cosily cramped, its two armchairs with antimacassars, its brass fender with fire-irons laid out, its ornaments and photographs, flowered wallpaper with a frieze.

She went there now. It smelt pleasantly of summer must, and slightly of soot. Drooping in a white jug on the single windowsill, pink roses were scentless and she took the withered blooms to the kitchen and rinsed the jug out, then went to cut fresh ones from the trellis in the garden at the front. When she had arranged them she fed the hens in the run and collected what eggs there were. She pumped up the back tyre of her bicycle because the valve was faulty. Not that she was going anywhere today.

Content but for her childlessness, Ellie did not complain if time hung heavy when her husband was in the fields. There was the routine of work and once a week she cycled the four and a half miles to Rathmoye with the eggs she regularly delivered, more often if there was further shopping to be done. She loved the journey through the empty countryside, and liked being in the town when she reached it, the bustle when the streets were busy, the different air. She liked being known by the shop people, being greeted by the man with the deaf-aid in English's hardware, sitting on her own at a table in Meagher's Café, paying in any cheques there were at the bank, searching for what she wanted in the Cash and Carry. More often than was always necessary, she made another confession. More often than she might have chosen, she heard the plot of the novel Miss Burke at the wool counter in Corbally's was reading. Old Orpen Wren greeted her, sometimes remembering who she was.

She hosed the dairy out, turned the milk buckets she'd

earlier scoured upside down on the slate draining-shelf beside the dairy sink. She put down poison in one of the turf sheds and in the feed shed, where something had been nibbling.

In her vegetable patch she weeded the parsley and thinned her carrots, saving what she pulled out. Tomorrow or the day after, the first of the peas she'd sown might be full enough to pick.

*

When Dillahan had moved his water line to the hill land he drove the tractor, its trailer behind it, down to the river-field. The fence he intended to replace was sagging, gaps here and there in the slack sheep-wire, a few of the posts rotten in the ground. Disturbed by his arrival, his ewes huddled together in the middle of the field before they processed back to the shade of the alders that grew randomly on both riverbanks, occasionally in the water. His sheepdogs settled down, in the shade too.

He wrenched out the staples that secured the barbed wire and the sheep-wire. They came out easily, but even so the work was slow – twenty-two new posts to be driven in, the old ones dug out if they had to be, the wire replaced. It would take him what remained of the morning, and longer after that than he'd thought, maybe even another hour tomorrow.

The time of year was difficult for Dillahan: it was in June seven years ago that the tragedy which had left him both widowed and childless had occurred. Try as he would, he could never prevent the memory from nagging when another June came, and lingering then until summer was finished with and the days were different. It was an October – sixteen months after the accident – when his mother had died, leaving him entirely on his own.

His sisters had found him Ellie. Not telling him, they went down to Templeross, having heard about Cloonhill. They put it to him afterwards in the kitchen, explaining about the institution they'd visited and repeating what he knew: that both of them being married, neither was free to take their mother's place on the farm. They had already failed in their search for a housekeeper, but did not now see it as failure, since instead of the older woman they were looking for, at Cloonhill they had been offered someone younger, experienced in domestic duties and prepared to take on some farm work: all that seemed more suitable. His sisters handed him a reference from the Reverend Mother in Templeross and he read it while his sisters were silent. When he put it down they said he wouldn't do better.

Fragments of all this, and what followed the arrangement he had agreed to, floated about Dillahan's thoughts as his sledgehammer drove in the first of the corner posts. 'There's not many as lucky,' he'd heard one of his sisters say in a telephone call that was made to Cloonhill, and hadn't known whether it was he or the girl who was referred to. He'd heard himself called a decent man, a man you could trust in the circumstances that had come about, a man who didn't miss Mass no matter what. Then his older sister drove away to collect the girl and brought her to the farm, her belongings in a white wooden box that had to be returned.

Dillahan was sunburnt, with reddish hair, the skin of his forehead and face freckled, his physical strength suggested by his features and his bulk. Since inheriting the farm he had managed on his own because he wanted to, hiring men only to help with the baling, a few days in September. His land was good, his acreage small; he rented grazing when it was required. He had worked nowhere else and had never wanted to.

He supported the corner post so that it would take the strain of the wire. Two strands of barbed above the squared sheep-wire were necessary if ever he put heifers in the river-field. He attached the second length, keeping it taut with the iron claw he used. He hammered in a staple and then another before he released the claw. He had to move out of the shade and the sun was hot now. His shirt was damp with sweat, a rash of nettle stings reddening one forearm.

Again the accident was there, suddenly, the way it always came. The thump there'd been, the moment of bewilderment, the sun in the yard as fierce as it was today, the moment of realizing. As best he could, he pushed it all away. 'We'll try her so,' he'd said to his sisters, and they'd said he should drive with them to Cloonhill so that he could see what he was getting, but he hadn't wanted to do that. 'She'll be all right,' he'd said.

He went to the trailer for more posts and carried them to the riverbank one by one. He drove her into Rathmoye when the shopping was more than usual, too heavy or bulky for a bicycle; he didn't begrudge her the time. He would have kept her company at the funeral yesterday except that he had never got to know Mrs Connulty as she had, delivering the Friday egg order. She hadn't minded being there on her own, she said, and had brought him back the news, as she always did: who had been at the funeral Mass and what they'd said in English's about the raddle powder that was ordered and still hadn't come in. Not for an instant did he imagine, the day she had arrived, that another day would come when he'd marry her, that he'd stand beside her and hear the same words said again, that afterwards he'd have his hand shaken as a husband. The wedding decorations were as they'd been before, the same advertisement for Winter's Tale sherry on mirrored glass, the noise and laughter, confetti strewn. ''Tis better so, 'tis better,' an old farmer he'd known all his life lowered his voice to approve when there was a private moment, each of them taking a corner at the urinals out the back. He sang for them at the wedding party, for her too, as everyone there knew. They went to Lahinch for three days afterwards, the farm looked after by one of the Corrigans. She'd never seen the sea before.

3

Florian Kilderry skimmed a pebble on the dark surface of water as still as ice. It bounced only once; twice, then three times when he tried again. The silence of early morning was unbroken, the air refreshingly cold. The bird he had been unable to identify this summer wasn't there again and he waited for it, hoping it would suddenly appear, swooping in just above the water in its particular way. He looked in the sky, but there was still no sign of it. His dog, a black Labrador, no longer young, looked also, her manner suggesting that she knew what for. These days she didn't do much on her own.

It took an hour to walk around the lake. Here and there a detour had to be made if the land was sodden, but it wasn't this morning. The upturned boat was still forgotten on the shingle where the stream trickled in, hardly trickling at all now. The reeds flourished best close to the water. They hadn't been cut for years.

When, in the past, there'd been parties – when people had driven down from Dublin – there was always the walk around the lake, whole processions of people and Florian among them, the child of the house. Cars were parked on the gravel turn-about: battered Dodges and Fords, the solitary Morgan that always came, Morrises and Austins. The emblem on the bonnet distinguished each and he knew the number plates, remembering them from the last time.

At night when there were parties he had never wanted to go to sleep, the music and the laughter always faintly reaching him in his bedroom. In the morning he crept about the house through silence that felt as if it would never cease.

Florian Kilderry – called Florian after a grandfather he hadn't known – was the sole relic of an Italian mother and an Anglo-Irish father, a couple whose devotion to one another had illuminated a marriage in which their foibles were indulged and their creditors charmed as part of everyday life. His mother had been a Verdecchia of Genoa, his father born into an army family originally of County Galway but long established in Somerset. The well-to-do Verdecchias had not approved of their daughter's romance with a wandering soldier who had become separated from his regiment as war was ending in 1918 and was certainly not aristocratic, as they themselves were. *Soldato di ventura* was the term that expressed their distaste; and too much, otherwise, was said, causing Natalia Verdecchia – several years younger than her suitor – to marry surreptitiously and flee with him to Ireland. 'I was never more than penniless,' Florian's father used to say, and was particularly so at that time, having managed to live from hand to mouth since his right leg was severely injured during the Battle of the Lys. But in spite of the Verdecchias' displeasure, in time there was a Genoese legacy – less than it might have been but enough to buy the house where the Kilderrys were to live for the remainder of their lives, where their only child was born and which on his father's recent death he had inherited.

Shelhanagh it was called, a country house of little architectural distinction, looking down on its own wide lake, two miles from Greenane Crossroads, five from the town of Castledrummond. It was now in a state of some decay, for in the Kilderrys' lifetime there had rarely been money to pay for its structural upkeep; and with the house itself, Florian had inherited a mass of debts and ongoing legal disputes. His father had been skilful to the end at procrastinating when the bills came in, good at knowing which to pay and which to leave. Florian was not. He had had no success at keeping things going, at growing vegetables to sell or coaxing plums from the trees before they fell and were lost in the long grass. The telephone had recently been cut off, cheques were referred back to him. Regularly a debt collector called.

Had the circumstances been less difficult, Florian would have remained for ever at Shelhanagh, but since there was no indication that anything would change and since he knew he did not possess the courage to suffer the indignities of poverty on his own, he had decided to take the advice he was offered, to sell the house and – child of exiles as he was – to become an exile himself. A fortnight ago the clergyman in Castledrummond had signed his application for a passport.

Born into the solitude of an only child, he had passed undemandingly through the years of early youth and those that followed it to become in manhood temperamentally hardly different from the boy he'd been: a polite, unpretending presence, given to reticence. 'He's shy a little of himself,' Natalia Kilderry in her lifetime often commented, though with the affection that always

27

accompanied a reference to her child. They were an affectionate family.

In his walk this morning Florian stood still for a moment, looking back at the tranquil orderliness of the lake. Then he made his way to the garden, high with artichokes that had become weeds among elder growth and convolvulus, and raspberry shoots that flourished only to be stifled, and last year's apples rotting where they lay. Beyond this lush wasteland there was a small cobbled yard. He passed through it and entered his unlocked house by the back door.

In the kitchen he made coffee and toasted bread. He didn't hurry. Reading *The Beautiful and the Damned*, he lingered over the last of the coffee and his first cigarette of the day. Then he washed some of the clothes that had accumulated and hung them out to dry among the plum trees. He tried to repair the water pump but again didn't succeed, as he'd known he wouldn't. From the kitchen, he heard what the postman had brought clattering through the letter-box and dropping on to the stone-paved floor. Passing through the hall a few minutes later, he found only brown-enveloped bills and threw them away unopened.

'She'll fetch a bit, I'd reckon,' the man from the estate agents' office had said when he'd finished with his tape-measure; and the Bank of Ireland thought so too. With the debts paid, there would be enough to live on, if not in splendour at least in comfort for a while. Enough to be a stranger somewhere else, although Florian didn't yet know where. He had never been outside Ireland.

Upstairs, he went about the rooms, assessing what

might be of interest to dealers. There was a lot less than once there'd been because during his last years his father had begun to sell the furniture, as already he had sold Shelhanagh's gorse-laden rocky little fields. But even without much furniture, here and there the house's better days held on. Pictures that had once cheered the walls were no more than a deeper shade of wallpaper now; yet each, for Florian, was perfectly a reminder. Ewers and the flowery bowls they'd stood in, washstands and dressing-tables, were gone, but he remembered where they had belonged and how they'd been arranged. Stale sunshine in the air had always been a summer smell and was again; the Schubert pieces his Italian cousin played when she came to Shelhanagh echoed; voices murmured. A ceiling had given way above the windows of a bedroom not slept in since the time of the parties, specks of plaster clinging to its threadbare carpet, the flies of some other summer darkening its windowsills. His father's typewriter, an antique Remington, was on a rickety table in an alcove, where his diaries were also, stacked in a corner.

Walls bulged with damp. On the bare boards of the landing a disconnected telephone receiver lay in the dust, separated from its cradle. Sunlight on dingy windowpanes cast shadows where the party people had danced, even in the afternoon. Music came from a big brash radiogram and they danced all over the house, in all the downstairs rooms, on the landing, in the hall. They had sat about on the stairs.

In the bedroom that had always been his he pulled the crumpled bedclothes up and covered the untidiness with a bedspread. It was a treachery, of course, his selling the house; he knew it was. A few days before his death, his father had reiterated what so often he had said before: that if desperate measures were called for a few of Shelhanagh's eighteen rooms could be let, and something made of the attractions of the lake and the surrounding tranquillity; that no matter how Florian wished to live, Shelhanagh would always at least be a roof above his head. 'Never betray your gift, beau,' his mother, ignoring practicalities, had earlier advised. For being the child of gifted parents – both of them watercolourists of exceptional skill – it was assumed that he would inherit, in some manner, to some degree, their talent.

Art had been their passion. Their easels and their brushes, their repeated views of the lake, their birds and flowers and city streets, their still-life compositions, ruled their lives and were the heart of Shelhanagh while they lived, and of themselves, and somehow of their marriage. The parties they gave had all to do with this, their guests mostly painters also or in some other way involved in the world of art, the sale of a picture often the reason for celebration.

That Florian would one day have a place in this world was cherished as an expectation. Presumed with unques-tioned certainty that its realization would come about, the prediction influenced his childhood, as his parents' love of one another did, and their kindness. But while accepting good intentions' generosity, he had his private doubts, his first experience of this occurring on the morn-ing of his fifth birthday.

Receiving the flat, black tin box he'd been given, he had

imagined it contained sweets until he folded back the hinged lid and saw the colours. His mother read out the names: chrome yellow and Prussian blue, madder and crimson lake, cobalt and emerald. He got them muddled; they said that didn't matter. 'Oh, you can, of course you can,' they said when they dipped the brush in the water and gave it to him. They showed him how; he splashed and made a mess. 'Of course you can,' they said again. He knew he couldn't.

This morning, going from one half-empty room to another, he found himself, without resentment, reflecting for longer than usual on such moments of spent time, and more reluctant than usual to accept the end that every day pressed closer. He stood in the doorway of the bedroom where his father had died while dressing himself and where – three years before that – his mother hadn't woken up on her sixty-first birthday. Now, only the wardrobe and the bed remained. 'Later on we'll see to the clothes,' his father had said, gathering together dresses and coats on their hangers, to be given to a charity he never made contact with, unable to bring himself to do it. His own clothes hung beside them now.

They couldn't help it, thinking the world of him. Florian knew that. Even then he almost had. Other forms of art had been suggested, and still – in spite of each negative outcome – the promise apparently remained, while he himself was aware only of failure. He minded at first, later much less. The house was full of books; he read a lot.

He didn't mind at all when the fees at his Dublin boarding-school were difficult to find and he had to leave it. An elderly tutor, a Mr Blades, arrived from Castle-drummond on a motorcycle every day for a while, until the same difficulty arose again and education ended. Then, or later, Florian might have left Shelhanagh, but he remained.

We do not press him to stay here with us, his father's untidy handwriting had recorded in an unposted letter. *We do not take upon ourselves the right to do so. But why waste a life behind a desk if it need not be wasted? There will be something, we say to one another, and know there will be: one day or another day there will be something. When that is ready to be discovered it shall be, because that is how things are. And he is happy in this house, finding his way.*

Florian never did. Instead, what he discovered, not long after his father's death, was an old Leica camera among the junk in one of the garden sheds. Picking it up, he pondered why, during all that searching the world of art for a niche he might have settled into, photography had not been mentioned. And when he tried the camera, to his surprise it worked.

He photographed Shelhanagh, its disrepair and melancholy atmosphere an attraction that afterwards in his photographs he invariably sought: today he intended to return to the burnt-out cinema where he'd been reprimanded for trespassing.

He completed before he did so the clearing of an attic choked with what had been put aside to throw away and never had been. His dog sniffed about in the dust, before lying down to wait for something better to happen. Not long ago she had gone with him on his photographic excursions, trotting behind his bicycle, but now she didn't want to. He carried what could be burnt to the bonfire that smouldered in the garden, then threw her tennis ball for her.

'See you mind the old place,' he instructed before he left and, lying down again, she beat her tail against the ground as if she understood. Jessie she was called.

4

Ellie Dillahan changed into her blue dress and almost immediately took it off again because the skirt needed to be ironed. She did that in the kitchen and when she was ready, when she'd smeared on lipstick and tidied her hair where the dress had mussed it, she wrote her list. Outside, she made sure the two trays of eggs on the carrier of her bicycle were secure and rode out of the yard with the basket for her shopping hanging empty on the handlebars.

She met no one, and there was still no sign of life at the grey cottage by the signpost, unoccupied since the Nelligans had had to be moved out. A Garda car was drawn up on the main road, as if there'd been an accident, two gardaí measuring skidmarks.

At the presbytery Father Millane himself answered the doorbell, the plump pinkness of his face broken into a smile. He said he'd have to get Mrs Lawlor before he noticed that Mrs Lawlor had left the egg money out on the ledge in the porch, which Ellie had been about to draw his attention to. While he was making sure it was right, he said he'd seen her at Mrs Connulty's funeral a week ago and said it was good of her.

'How're things with yourself, Ellie? The hay looking good, is it?'

Ellie said things were all right. Some of the hay was cut and still lying. It was plentiful this year.

'Grand!' Father Millane enthused. 'Isn't that grand!'

He often used the word. Noted in the town for his skills of persuasion and an ability to fix things, he it was who laid down the spiritual tenets by which Rathmoye's people lived their lives, his the voice that fiercely condemned all threats to the orderly Church he spoke for. Respected for his cloth and for himself, Father Millane rejoiced when the news brought to him by his parishioners was good. There was a lot to be thankful for, he regularly asserted; no matter which way you looked at it, that had to be said. This morning Ellie heard it said again; and, believing that she had herself a lot to be thankful for, was warm in her agreement.

Opening her hall door some minutes later, Miss Connulty repeated the sentiments of Father Millane when he'd said that Ellie had been good to attend the funeral.

'Ah well, I wouldn't not have, Miss Connulty. I'm only sorry I couldn't come back to the house. We had Mr Brennock that day. D'you know Mr Brennock at all?'

'I don't, to be honest.'

'He's the best of them with the cattle.'

It was the daily girl who'd been taking in the eggs for a long time, ever since Mrs Connulty had found the stairs too much. Only once or twice during the last year had Miss Connulty answered the doorbell: Ellie didn't know her all that well. Not that she'd known Mrs Connulty much better, but even so she wouldn't not have attended the funeral.

'I don't know what we'd do without you, Ellie,' Miss Connulty said, sounding like her mother. She remarked that it was a glorious day, which Father Millane had said also. 'Now, whoever's that?' she interrupted herself.

Ellie turned round.

'Just after crossing from Matthew Street,' Miss Connulty said, and Ellie saw the man who'd asked her for directions on the morning of the funeral. He was wheeling a bicycle through the parked cars and was occasionally obscured by them.

'Whoever's that?' Miss Connulty said again.

Ellie took the money that had been held out to her before Miss Connulty's attention was distracted. 'Thanks, Miss Connulty,' she said.

'That's never the chap taking photographs at the funeral, Ellie? Did you see him there?'

Ellie nodded, then said she had.

'A few people noticed him,' Miss Connulty said. 'They said a tweed suit. Did you see him taking the photographs, Ellie?'

'I did, all right.'

'Wasn't that peculiar, though?'

Ellie said she'd thought so herself. She remembered the dark hair flopping across the forehead, the serious gaze when he'd asked whose funeral it was, the smile when it came, the colourful tie. She remembered noticing the hands that operated the camera. Delicate hands, she'd said to herself.

'I thought he'd be instructed to take the photographs.'

'Why would he be?'

'It's only I thought that. He was asking where the picture house was.'

'What'd he want with the picture house?'

'I don't know.'

'Was he wanting to go to the pictures? Didn't he know the picture house is burnt down?'

'I'd say he knew the state of it, all right.'

'Where's he off to now for himself?' Miss Connulty asked, when the figure they had been watching mounted his bicycle and rode off towards Cashel Street.

'The same next Friday is it, Miss Connulty?'

'Oh, the same'll do nicely.'

Miss Connulty said she had the beds to make yet and shouldn't be standing here. Ellie said goodbye and went on.

In English's the raddle powder still hadn't come in. The man with the deaf-aid went to look and shook his head from the other end of the counter. She said it didn't matter and wondered if he could hear and thought he probably couldn't. 'Tuesday,' he called after her when she began to go, and then remembered that Friday was her day for being in the town and raised a hand apologetically. She understood.

She left her bicycle in Cloughjordan Road, against the railings of the church. She had to wait a while before a priest was there to hear her confession, but she didn't mind. Her penance wasn't much. She lit a candle before she left.

*

'The Connultys owned it,' the woman in Meagher's Café said when Florian asked her about the catastrophe at the cinema. 'Well, of course they still do.'

She was a big woman, broad-shouldered, her black hair in a net. Her chapped fingers and reddened, windswept face suggested a farmer's wife, hard-working, butter churned in an icy-cold dairy, exposure to all weathers. She had joined Florian at a table in the window, since no table was unoccupied and there was room at his. When she began to talk to him he had marked his place in *The Beautiful and the Damned* and pushed the dog-eared paperback to one side.

'You'd remember it?' he asked. 'The fire?'

'Oh, I do, I do.'

The waitress brought a pot of tea. She'd be back with cakes, she said.

'And boiling water,' the woman called after her. 'Bring boiling water.'

There hadn't been anyone in the office at the coal yards when Florian went there to get permission to take photographs. No one had come while he waited, but there were keys hanging from a rack on the wall and when he asked in the yard a man shovelling coal picked out one with 'Coliseum' on the label and handed it to him. Miss O'Keeffe was taking the post over to Mr Connulty in the public house, he said. 'Be sure you'll put that key back when you've done,' he instructed, and Florian promised. For an hour he'd prowled about the blackened void. Tattered curtains still hung where the screen had been, the seats were metal skeletons, the balcony had collapsed. He imagined actors' voices continuing in the clamour of panic, and laughter, music playing. It was a desolate place.

'A cigarette thrown down,' the woman in the café said, stirring sugar into her tea. 'Only the one life taken, but you'd miss the old picture house.'

'There's a poster still intact.'

'There used be posters in frames on the stairway, going up to the balcony. Spencer Tracy, Mickey Rooney. Joan Crawford.'

'It's Norma Shearer who's left.'

'God, Norma Shearer!'

The first time she had been in the Coliseum it was to see *Du Barry Was a Lady*. 'Tommy Dorsey,' she said. 'It wasn't long opened then.'

The waitress came with the cakes and Florian took a slice of jam roll. The background music reached the end of its tape and began again.

'I can't touch a sweet thing,' the woman said.

Meagher's Café was at the junction of Cashel Street and Cloughjordan Road and from the window there was a view of the Church of the Most Holy Redeemer. Occasionally the woman who shared Florian's table waved to someone on the street or rapped on the glass.

'You mightn't know,' she said, 'it was old Mr Connulty was the one taken in the fire.'

'No, I didn't know that.'

'His wife lived after, nearly seventeen years. We buried her the other week.'

'I think I noticed that funeral.'

'Oh, you would have in Rathmoye, you wouldn't have missed it. Mr Connulty took to the drink after a trouble they had in the family. Of an evening, when he wouldn't want to go home with a drop too much taken, he'd settle himself at the back of the balcony and he'd get left there all night if they didn't shine the torch on him. Well, you can guess it then – the place went up like a box of matches and they overlooked him. Am I too loquacious for you?'

'No, not at all.'

He offered the woman a cigarette, but she refused it.

'Oh, go ahead,' she said when he hesitated before he lit one for himself.

The Leica was on the table, the leather on it stained and torn, its strap repaired with black insulating tape. The woman had displayed no curiosity about it; nor had she enquired what Florian's purpose in the cinema had been. She had been courted on that same balcony, she said.

'Saturday nights, a construction man from north Cork. He said he'd build me a palace, but I didn't marry him all the same.'

The man she'd married instead had brought her out to where his farm was, his father's at the time. She'd been there since, seven children. The youngest one had the makings of a Christian Brother, she said, not that anything was mentioned yet.

'You'd miss the old picture house,' she said again.

She went soon after that but Florian didn't open his book. In the destroyed cinema, quite suddenly, he had found himself wondering why he hadn't known that photography would fail him also, or he it; why he hadn't known that the images he achieved were too slight, each one too ordinary a statement. But perhaps he had known and failed to make much of it, even particularly to notice? And did it matter, now that so much was over for him, and disappointment's sting had long ago been drawn?

On the street outside, two women greeted one another and paused for a moment to talk. A van, drawn up to deliver bread, drove off. Figures in the far distance descended the steep church steps.

'Were you wanting your bill?' the waitress asked, coming to the table with her empty tray.

He paid, counting out the coins when he was handed what was scribbled for him.

'See you again,' the waitress said.

*

Ellie finished in Corbally's, delayed for a while by Miss Burke. Then she cycled down to the Cash and Carry.

People were talking about the weather, saying they were getting a great summer. She had heard that already in Magennis Street, and Father Millane and Miss Connulty had said it. She took a cardboard box from the pile by the door and called over to the counter girl she'd recently got to know. She had sugar to get, and creamery butter and cornflour, sultanas or raisins, whichever were there, sixty-watt bulbs. Not more than that; she wouldn't be late back, easily by twelve.

She went to get the electric bulbs, picking up a packet of Rinso on the way. She was on the way to the sugar shelf when she saw the photographer again, looking for something he wanted, his back to her before he turned and saw her too.

5

Orpen Wren waited at Rathmoye's railway station, as every morning he did, and again every evening. He waited in all seasons without impatience: this morning, being summery and warm, it was a pleasure and he allowed himself to doze, knowing that the sound of the advancing Dublin train would rouse him. But no train came, and had not since the railway station's closure, and would not ever again.

Orpen Wren lived in both the present and the past. He had long ago been employed to catalogue the library of the St Johns of Lisquin, and in a sense had never left that house, although the St Johns, thirty-two years ago, had put their estate on the market and auctioned their furniture. The renowned St John library, for generations visited by scholars, was pillaged by dealers, the remnants they rejected thrown on to a fire in the yard when the house was emptied and its roof stripped of lead and slates. Mantelpieces and ceilings, doors and panelling, the balconies that had curved on either side of the stairs as a feature of the wide first-floor landing, were taken out and put aside to be sold. The ruined shell was razed, tons of stone carted away to be sold also.

More than three years after these events the librarian had arrived in Rathmoye one frosty November morning. It was said that he had been emotionally affected by what he'd witnessed and had since wandered the roads; but this was not known as fact. He stated himself that he had never left Lisquin, that he alone had always been there, yet no habitation remained, not even rudimentary shelter from the weather.

Although in want and homeless, he had not been in low spirits when he first presented himself to the town; he was not now. Declaring that he would be content in whatever accommodation there was, he had been given one of the alms dwellings in St Morpeth's Terrace, which were in poor repair, only a few fit for occupation. He afterwards showed his gratitude by regularly repeating on the streets that he was happy in Rathmoye, while never ceasing to speak of the great house as if it were still standing. Among his modest items of luggage were what became known in the town as the St John papers, which he declared had been temporarily entrusted to him. He carried them on his person and every day, at the railway station or on the streets, was ready to pass them back to a member of the St John family or any Lisquin servant who might return now that the family's fortunes had been restored. He was also in possession at all times of an entitlement to a state pension. It wasn't much, but was enough.

Age had rendered Orpen Wren skinny, the flesh fallen in from the bones of his face, hollows like caverns beneath his wasted chin, eyes that had become pinpricks in the depths. Clothes hung loosely on his limbs, buttons missing from the threadbare overcoat he always wore; tattered brown shoes were in need of better heels and soles. Even this morning in the sun at the railway station, he had a frozen look.

His journey from St Morpeth's Terrace had taken him past the Protestant church, called after St Morpeth also and distinguished by its dark, slender spire and ancient gravestones, past the Church of the Most Holy Redeemer, limestone bright, with space for parking, and a pietà separating its second and third flights of steps. The one-time librarian had entered St Morpeth's, as he always did, and stayed for fifteen minutes.

When no train arrived – or when, in Orpen Wren's belief, one arrived and went on without putting down any passengers – he set out on his walk back to the town, the shops beginning when he reached Irish Street. He paused at the windows in case a display had changed overnight. None had: drapers' dummies were as they had been since early spring, the spectacles on an optician's cardboard faces had been the same for longer. Pond's beauty aids were still reduced, travel bargains still offered, interest rates steady.

In Magennis Street a steel keg was being rolled to a pavement aperture. The tall assistant from McGovern's, white-aproned, with glasses, was talking to a van driver. *Yorkshire Relish, Thick. 12 Bottles*, the printing on a carton in the van driver's arms declared. Renowned for his resemblance to de Valera, the tall assistant ticked off the item on an order sheet and said there should be something from Mi Wadi.

A cat came creeping into Orpen's legs, rubbing itself against his shins, and he bent down to stroke its silky black head. He knew this cat and enjoyed its company. But, as abruptly as always, it lost interest and slinked away.

'Wait till I'll get it for you.' The tall assistant greeted

him from the shop doorway, hurrying back to the tea counter even while he spoke. He opened one drawer and then another, eventually finding an envelope on a mahogany shelf between two tall Oriental canisters in which coffee beans were stored. 'Well, that was great,' he said, alluding to a reference to McGovern's in the letter he had been lent.

'You noticed it?'

'Oh, I did, I did.'

'Would Mr McGovern remember the occasion?'

'To tell you the truth, he said he didn't.'

The documents that were carried twice a day to the railway station – notes kept of births and deaths, receipts for burial charges at the Church of Ireland graveyard at Lisquin, papers relating to the purchase or sale of land, records of maintenance and repairs at the house – made turgid reading for the most part. But there were a few personal letters that were of greater interest, that touched upon life during the years of Lord Townshend's viceroyalty, or related details of the rebellion of 1798, or told of the Famine years. In shops Orpen sometimes left one for perusal.

Carefully now, he tucked what had been returned to him into his clothes and continued on his way. Sometimes his name eluded him, but returned when it was used by someone on the streets, or by the post-office clerks when he went to collect his pension. They chided him in the post office because the greater part of what he received there was given away to the tinker girls who held out to him their rag-wrapped infants, or was dropped into the palms of the tramps who now and again passed through the town, or slipped to shame-faced men who mumbled tales of misfortune and bad luck.

Greeted by none of these this morning, Orpen reached the Square, where cars were untidily parked and a woman in an overall was sweeping the pavement outside Bodell's Bar. Windows bore the names of solicitors and accountants on pebbled glass or sunburnt mesh; more brashly, various other services were offered. The brass plates of doctors and the town's dentist had for the most part lost their pristine shine; a fortnightly chiropodist relied for custom on a handwritten postcard beside his bell. Hall doors were green or red, black or shades of blue.

One house was derelict. Weeds sprouted from chutes that had rusted, an aerial drooped crookedly from the masonry of a chimney-stack. But next door a credit company was spruce and, further on, the steps and pillars of the grey courthouse struck an important note, although today no court was in session.

The curator of the St John papers rested on the seat beside the Square's tribute to a rebel hero, a resolute, shirt-sleeved figure with his right arm raised in a gesture of command, the unfurled flag he held draping folds of bronze over the stone of his monument's pedestal. Whenever he was in the Square, Orpen rested on this seat, the colours of the hall doors impinging a little on his reflections, the derelict house occasionally seeming hostile. He watched Mr Hassett from the bank making his way in the direction of Bodell's Bar. There were references in the papers to the bank when it had been the Valley Hotel: how the St John family of that time had left their trap or dog-cart in the hotel yard when they came in to Rathmoye.

Mr Hassett entered the public house after he had paused to speak to the woman sweeping the pavement. Orpen watched the daily girl polishing the brass on the hall door of the Connultys' bed-and-breakfast house and when a moment later he noticed a stranger in the Square there was no mistaking, even in the distance, the St John straight back and assured comportment. This would be old George Freddie's grandson, born after the family had gone. George Anthony he'd been christened.

Orpen Wren stood up, saying to himself as soon as he had a clearer view that this was definitely George Anthony. When he saluted him across the Square the stranger didn't notice at first, and when he did he hesitated. Then Florian Kilderry raised a hand in response.

6

'Come on out of that.' Dillahan called up his dogs and they came at once when they saw him going to the Vaux-hall, not the tractor. The front tyre that was leaking air a bit hadn't lost much, but he put the pump in the back any-way in case it played up. Then he drove over to Crilly, where once in a while it was necessary to round up his mountain sheep, to count them and look for any that might have strayed. It was the only time the dogs ever entered the car and they always knew. As much as he did himself, they liked the mountainy land.

He was delayed there because an old ewe had died. He might have left her in the heather, but he found a place that was a better grave for what remained of her. He wasn't sentimental, but he respected sheep.

He watched his two dogs working them, gathering them and driving them in his direction, holding them while he counted. Misty earlier, the sky had cleared. Fluffy white clouds moved gently; patches of blue appeared in the grey. He didn't have to climb higher than the begin-ning of the rock-face.

He drove the Vauxhall slowly down from Crilly, past Gortduff and Baun. He stopped by the gate into a field he was hoping to buy. Its acquisition would make his days easier because of the access through it to his river land, the long way round no longer necessary. He liked the tidiness of that as much as the prospect of increasing the extent of his farm and restoring the field to good heart: Gahagan had let it go.

He left the car in the yard but didn't go into the house. He hadn't expected to be back from Crilly so soon or he would have said he'd have something to eat in the kitchen instead of taking sandwiches today. The dogs went with him when he took the tractor to the lower hill fields.

*

Ellie pulled the sheets of newspaper back, then knelt on them again, applying more Cardinal polish to the scullery floor. She hadn't ever used Cardinal before, but the concrete surface had been that same red once; she could tell because there were traces of it left behind. The whole scullery looked brighter when she'd finished.

In the kitchen she ran water into a kettle. When it boiled she made tea in the small teapot she used when she was alone. She thought of poaching an egg, but she didn't because she wasn't hungry.

She sat in the yard on one of the kitchen chairs, with her tea and the *Nenagh News*. A pickaxe had been found in the boot of a car when its driver was arrested, declared drunk. Ore had been discovered near Toomyvara; Killeen's Pride had won twice at Ballingarry. Top prices were being paid for ewes.

The newspaper slipped from her fingers and she didn't pick it up. She shouldn't have liked the photographer smiling at her. She shouldn't have said she'd show him when he said what he was after was chicken-and-ham paste. She had walked about the Cash and Carry with a stranger she didn't know. She had told him her name. 'Nothing,' she'd said when he asked her what Ellie was short for. He laughed and she wanted to laugh herself and didn't know why.

She picked up the newspaper from where it had fallen on to the concrete surface. She carried the chair and the tray back to the kitchen, the newspaper carelessly folded under one arm. She threw away the dregs in the teapot and washed up her cup and saucer.

'Hullo,' a voice called out in the yard.

She hadn't heard a car. It would be Mrs Hadden for her buttermilk. It was the day she came and she never drove in, preferring to park in the road because she found it difficult to negotiate the turn into the gateway.

Grateful for the distraction, yet resenting it, Ellie pushed the kettle on to the hot ring in case Mrs Hadden wanted tea. She came to the front door, which no one else ever did. 'I mustn't disturb you,' she always said when Ellie opened it and she said it now. Ellie led her to the kitchen.

'A cup of tea?' she offered, and Mrs Hadden said no, not adding, as she was inclined to, that she was on a diuretic and had to watch it. What she liked instead of tea was a soda bun if buns were cooling on a wire rack.

Ellie apologized because there were no buns today. She fetched the buttermilk from the scullery, in one of the two jars Mrs Hadden provided herself, and Mrs Hadden began to fish coins out of her purse, at the same time reporting on the condition of an aunt who'd been taken into a home.

'Heart-rending,' she said. 'Not that it isn't a lively place. It's the quiet ones you'd be suspicious of.'

There was more, about homes that had been, or should

be, closed down because of casualness as regards sedating drugs. 'It'll come to all of us, of course,' Mrs Hadden said.

'Yes, it will.'

'I had an uncle-in-law who refused point blank to go in anywhere. Horry Gould.'

Horry Gould had gone on to reach a hundred and one. He had bought a new suit of clothes every birthday for the last ten years of his life. Another way of being defiant, Mrs Hadden said.

'The day before he went, he was singing "The Wild Colonial Boy" in his bed.'

Mrs Hadden had another aunt, who embroidered purses, but attacks of rheumatism increasingly interfered with that. Ellie had heard before about this curtailment and was now brought up to date, the news being that the affliction eased a little in the summer months.

'Small mercies,' Mrs Hadden conceded. 'We'd call it that, I suppose.'

'Yes.'

His own name was a mouthful, he'd said: Florian Kilderry. His face crinkled up a bit when he laughed and sometimes it did when he smiled. 'You'd know everyone in Rathmoye?' he'd said, the girl at the counter listening. He had walked out of the Cash and Carry beside her.

'It's a legend in the family,' Mrs Hadden said. 'Singing songs in your bed at a hundred and one!'

'Yes.'

Because it was heavy, he said when he took the carrier bag from her, and it wasn't heavy at all. His bicycle was called a Golden Eagle, an eagle on the upright of the handlebars. She'd never seen a bicycle called that before and she wondered if it was special even though the mud-guards were battered and looked old.

'We saw old Horry into his grave at Ardrony.'

Lost for a moment in the conversation, Ellie nodded anyway, covering her confusion by saying it was good, the summer being a better time for rheumatism. 'It's only a handful of people I'd know in Rathmoye,' she'd said when they were standing outside in the sun, and he said of course. He offered her a cigarette.

'Are you well yourself, Ellie?' Mrs Hadden stood up, say-ing she was on her way.

'Oh, I am,' Ellie said, and wondered if Mrs Hadden had noticed something before she remembered that this was a question she was always asked.

'It's good you're well, Ellie.'

They walked to the yard together, and on to where the car was parked, drawn in to the narrow verge of the road.

'Next week I could be late,' Mrs Hadden said.

The car was backed slowly, and a little way into the yard gateway, before it was turned. Mrs Hadden settled herself and waved from the window she'd wound down. Ellie stood in the gateway, listening to the sound of the car's engine until it was no longer there. Cow-parsley was limp among faded foxgloves on the verges of the road. A field-mouse scampered and disappeared. The last of the dust disturbed by the car tyres settled.

If he was there again in Rathmoye she would cross the street. If he spoke to her she would say she had to get on. She would be ashamed confessing it because it was silly, because all she had to do was to think of something else when he came into her mind. But now, when she tried to, she couldn't. She kept seeing him, standing against packets of Bird's jelly in the Cash and Carry, tins of mustard, Saxa salt. As if they meant something, they were stuck in her mind, as if they were more than they could possibly be, and she wondered if they would ever be the same again, if what she'd bought herself would be, the Brown and Polson's cornflour, Rinso. She wondered if she would be the same herself; if she was no longer – and would not be again – the person she was when she had gone to Mrs Connulty's funeral and for all the time before that. When he had asked whose funeral it was it had been the beginning but she hadn't known. When Miss Connulty had drawn her attention to him in the Square she had realized. When he'd smiled in the Cash and Carry she'd known it too. She had been different already when she stood with him in the sunshine, when he offered her the cigarette and she shook her head. Anyone could have seen them and she hadn't cared.

In the house she put on her farm clothes, a brown overall and wellington boots. She collected the milk buckets and the cans from the dairy and scoured them at the kitchen sink. She hosed the dairy, then brushed the surplus of water into the shallow drain. She laid the buckets and the cans, the scoops and measures, on the long concrete shelf, each in its own position, as she'd once been shown. She couldn't do anything when first she'd come: she couldn't tell the breeds of sheep; she'd never collected eggs or cleaned a henhouse, or tethered a goat. She hadn't known a man before, except for priests and a few workmen and delivery men, and then only knowing them to see, hardly more than that. The first time she'd seen shaving soap turning into a lather that the razor scraped away she'd been astonished. She'd never sat down opposite a man across a table from her. But before she became a wife, when she was still a servant, she was used to everything, except the sharing of a bed.

In the crab-apple orchard the hens ran freely, a few of them clustered beneath the trees, a black one pecking near a tractor tyre that had been split to make a feeder for lambs but had somehow found a place there. On the dry, hard ground there was hardly a blade of grass left. When winter came, grass would grow again; it always did. Fourteen more eggs had been laid and she collected them in the cracked brown bowl that had become part of her daily existence. Closing the gate again when she left the crab-apple orchard, she slipped the loop of chain over the gate-post. He had a way of hesitating before he spoke, of looking away for a moment and then looking back. He had a way of holding a cigarette. When he'd offered her one he'd tapped one out of the packet for himself and hadn't lit it. The rest of the time he was with her he'd held it, unlit, between his fingers.

Slowly, both hands clasped round the brown egg-bowl, she returned to the house. In the kitchen she mixed Kia-Ora Orange with water as cold as it would come, filling a plastic bottle to the brim. She scraped potatoes and cut up a cabbage before she set off to the hillside land with her husband's drink.

It was the most distant part of the farm, twenty-two acres on the eastern slope and on the plateau of the unnamed hill, land separated from the rest of the farm-holding by coppices, through which the right-of-way track became an undergrowth, making it difficult for the tractor. He had been cutting it back, she noticed when she reached it, the summer shoots still scattered on the ground, overhead branches sawn. It wasn't worth it to possess a hedge-cutter, he maintained, with only a few hedges and this half-mile of advancing growth to contend with. On the way back from the top field he would tidy it up as he went; she remembered that from previous summers, piles of logs no more than an inch or so in diameter, and the place where he burnt the brushwood. It wasn't his obligation to keep the track clear; he did it to avoid an argument with Gahagan, who neglected it. Years ago, birch and ash had become as high as forest trees.

She tried to think about all that, to see before she came to it another blackened area, a different place from last time, his way of keeping the track clear. Badgers had been here once and he had shown her their setts. It was easier not to feel a stranger to herself here, to tell herself that she had allowed a convent-child's make-belief to have its way with her, to be ashamed and know it was right to be ashamed. It was easier because everything around her made sense in a way she understood. The confusion of thoughts that did not feel her own made no sense at all.

She took the short-cut from the boreen along one side of the small pasture, and passed into the gloom of the wood. He would try to buy the wood, her husband said, if ever it came up for sale, and she'd always hoped it would. Among the trees there was a stillness, without birds, rarely visited by the foxes which went to ground in the banks on either side of the track that petered out when the slope of the hill began. God's peace they would have called it at Cloonhill, Sister Clare and Sister Ambrose, and the Reverend Mother, who came out once in a while from Templeross. God was never not there for you, wherever you were, however you were. Every minute of your day, every minute of your life. There for your comfort, there to lift from you the awful burden of your sins. Only confess, only speak to God with contrition in your heart: God asked no more than that.

Unhurried in the wood, not wanting to hurry, Ellie reached out for these crowding memories. Cloonhill was gone now, closed down three years ago, the nuns gone back to the convent in Templeross. But you didn't lose touch with a place when it wasn't there any more; you didn't lose touch with yourself as you were when you were part of it, with your childhood, with your simplicity then. That had been said too, still was: Sister Ambrose sent a Christmas card and always put a letter in.

Sunshine began again, flickering through the trees. The two thick banks that protected the foxes' lairs were tightly grassed, grazed by some creature, hardly enough nourishment for more than one; the buttercups' long tendrils had been chopped away where the banks weren't there any more. The tractor tyres left no mark here; the gate to the hillside fields was open. She stood still for a moment, praying for the courage to confess, pleading for protection against her thoughts; and walking on, she remembered how the old priest at Templeross used to rap on the grille and tell you to speak up. *Hail, Mary, Mother of God, pray for us now* . . . No matter what, you always felt better after-wards.

From where she was the farmhouse, far down below, seemed remote, a place by itself with its yard and cluster of barns. People didn't come much to the house except for eggs or buttermilk, and her in-laws from Shinrone once a year, on a Sunday afternoon. You couldn't count the postman or the insurance man. You couldn't count the artificial-insemination man, or the man to read the meter. Nothing went by on the road except the Corrigans' tractor, or Gahagan looking for an animal that had strayed. 'Quiet,' they had said at Cloonhill, telling her about it. 'A quiet place.' She might be asked to wear a uniform, they had said, but that had never been a requirement. *It's not like you'd think*, she wrote in her first letter to Sister Ambrose. *More easygoing than that.*

'Ah, thanks,' her husband said, when she was near enough to hear, and reached out for the drink when she was closer. No more than a bit of tidying up, he said; a couple of places where the wire was gone, nothing like by the river. These few weeks of the year he came up every day to turn the grass as soon as he'd cut it. Since he was there, he repaired the fences at the top.

'Thanks,' he said again, keeping the bottle by him when he returned to his task, tightening and stapling, weaving in lengths of wire with pliers. Having greeted her, the two sheepdogs slipped back to where they'd chosen to lie.

'Mrs Hadden came,' she said.

*

Dillahan worked for another couple of hours and on the way back looked for Gahagan. He had already made an offer for the field he was after and Gahagan had said he'd think about it. But the pick-up wasn't in the yard and there was no response when he called out. Widowed for fifteen years, Gahagan lived alone, without help on the farm, and was often difficult to find.

Dillahan went on. He stopped to open a gate and drop the dogs off. Every evening now they drove in the cows on their own.

7

In the pantry he had converted to a darkroom Florian
Kilderry developed the Rathmoye photographs and took
them to the drawing-room, empty but for a trestle-table
and the radiogram no one had wanted to buy when his
father tried to sell it. Attached with drawing-pins to the
walls were watercolour sketches that had been there for
years: studies of a peregrine in flight, a picnic on a strand
with people bathing, tennis in a garden. Close together,
two actors conversed in an empty theatre. The leaves of a
tulip tree half obscured the blue façade of a house; a girl
gathered washing from a clothes line. At a street corner
the three-card trick was played on an opened-out
umbrella.

The watercolours were neither as fresh nor as bright as
once they'd been. Their paper had curled, was marked
with the ravages of flies, affected by sunburn and the rust
of the drawing-pins. But even so their faded dazzle belit-
tled the rows of photographs now laid out on the trestle-
table. That the camera had failed to convey movingly the
bleakness of another disaster was readily confirmed; and
with a feeling almost of relief Florian added these photographs to the pile he'd made of all the others.

On his way with them to his garden bonfire he was
interrupted by the doorbell and knew who it was. Books
were stacked against a wall in the hall, ready for the dealer

who had come when he'd said he would. A stranger to Florian, he was a restless man in a brown striped suit, with a narrow fringe of black moustache and a hat he didn't take off. He made a swift, cursory examination, repeatedly shaking his head. 'The Razor's Edge,' was his only comment. 'Not many'd read that today.'

'I would myself,' Florian mildly protested.

He couldn't have burnt the books; he couldn't have so casually destroyed the pages on which he had first encountered Miss Havisham and Mr Verloc, and Gabriel Conroy and Edward Ashburnham and Heathcliff, where first he'd glimpsed Netherfield Park and Barchester.

'I'm a sentimental reader,' he admitted to his visitor.

'A general disposal, would it be?'

'It would. I'll help you with them to your car.'

He had kept a few books back to read again while the house was being sold, which he assumed would take all summer.

'Ugly business, emptying a place,' the man remarked.

'Yes, it is.'

A modest payment was made and, alone again, Florian put a record on the radiogram. The needle slithered, a dance tune lost and then returning, a woman's husky voice. He turned the volume up and opened one of the drawing-room windows, picked up *The Beautiful and the Damned* from the trestle-table. Jessie padded behind him to the garden.

'Falling in love again,' the woman sang there too, and Florian lay on a patch of grass, his dog stretched out beside him. A tangle of wild sweet pea grew through berberis and fuchsia; deep scarlet peonies poked out of undergrowth. He lit a cigarette, and while the slurp of romance continued he wondered if Scandinavia might be the place of his exile.

The thought was not a new one. He had imagined Scandinavia before, uncluttered, orderly, the architecture of Sweden, Norwegian landscape, Finland in winter. He had seen himself – now saw himself again – in an out-of-the-way town, its houses clustered around a tidy square, a church's wooden spire. He had a room there, in its gaunt old hotel.

The music ceased, the whine of the needle on the empty centre of the record so faint it was hardly anything. Still dwelling on his exile, Florian finished his cigarette and stubbed it out on the grass. The sun was slipping away, the evening light becoming dusky. Jessie clambered to her feet when he did, went back with him to the drawing-room, where he lifted the needle off. In the kitchen he put sausages on to fry.

He had spoken to the girl in Rathmoye because, seeing her again, he had wanted to. When she'd led him to the shelf he was looking for her voice was soft and shy, unhurried, of the country. He had noticed first her grey-blue eyes, and while they talked had found himself liking, more and more, her unaffected features.

He carried his food, and Jessie's, back to the garden when the sausages were ready. The air was scented now, as often it was at this time. Not yet silent, the birds were quieter than they had been. Sometimes in the garden on a summer's evening he fell asleep and woke to the dampness of gathering dew. But tonight he knew he wouldn't.

She put on a light coat and a quaintly piquant Napoleon-hat of Alice-blue, he read in bed . . . *and they walked along the Avenue*

and into the Zoo, where they properly admired the grandeur of
the elephant and the collar-height of the giraffe, but did not visit
the monkey-house because Gloria said that monkeys smelt so
bad.

Hours later Florian dreamed of the Zoo, and the elephant's grandeur, and Gloria's hat. But Gloria was not
Gloria, she was his Italian cousin, Isabella, and then she
was the girl in Rathmoye. 'Lovely as an orchid,' his father
said the first time Isabella came to Shelhanagh, but when
he said it in the dream he meant the girl.

There were other dreams, but they faded into the darkness, passing outside memory, and when Florian woke,
just after dawn, it was his father's voice that still remained,
saying he meant the girl. And Florian's mother – without
insistence, which was particularly her way – said the bird
that came in the mornings to the lake was a squacco
heron. And somewhere there was Schubert on the piano.

Florian tried to sleep again, to make that dream go on,
which often as a child he had tried to do but never with
success. His dog was sleeping, undisturbed, on the landing beyond his bedroom door. The details of dreaming
blurred, then were gone.

Only Isabella had ever played the piano, which a week
ago had been taken from the house. She had been sent
from Genoa every summer to perfect her English, although
at Shelhanagh her English was considered to be as good as
anyone's. She always came in July, a child at first, younger
than Florian but not by much. He was suspicious, resentful of an invasion of his solitude; but growing closer as
they grew up, he and Isabella discovered in each other a
companionship neither had known before. His cousin was

assured, and knowledgeable in ways he wasn't, and teased a little. *'Nella sua mente c'é una gran confusione,'* she would say as if to herself, and he would shrug when, in translation, he heard himself called muddled. He knew he was, and Isabella only did because by then he told her everything. She lifted loneliness from him, making of the secrets he once had guarded from her curiosity secrets that belonged to both of them. *'Meraviglioso!'* she cried when he confided that on darkening winter evenings he had stolen out of his one-time boarding-school to follow people on the streets, making of each shadowy presence what he wished it to be. Hunched within themselves, his quarries hurried from their crimes, the pickpocket with his wallets and his purses, the bank clerk with embezzlement's gain kept safe beneath his clothes, the simple thief, the silent burglar. Sinister at dark hall doors, they took out latchkeys and, curtains drawn, a light went on. The blackmailer wrote his letters, the shoplifter cooked his purloined supper. Saviour of desperate girls, a nurse wiped clean her instruments. A dealer packaged dreams, a killer washed his hands. *'Magnifico!'* Isabella cried.

She brought a real world herself: Cesare and Enrico, Bartolomeo, Giovanni, a different snapshot pinned up each time she came. And Pietro Pallotta in evening dress, worshipped from afar, and Signor Canepaci of Credito Italiano. They broke her heart or she broke theirs; and Florian was her friend and always would be. 'You let me be myself,' she complimented him. Two halves of one they were, she used to say, her more precise Italian losing elegance in translation. He knew it was true: they complemented one another.

The dusk of early morning lightened. Florian slept again, and dreamed again but afterwards did not know he had. He didn't know when it was he had first loved Isabella and often thought he probably always had. 'We could be here,' she used to say, speaking of Shelhanagh and of the future. But love, for Isabella, did not come into it, and there'd been other girls because of that: pretty Rose Mary Darty, who lived not far away, and the girl in the chemist's in Castledrummond, Noeleen Fahy the station master's daughter, Ingrid Bergman in *For Whom the Bell Tolls*. There'd never been much, but what there was had always to do with Isabella – another hopeless effort to tidy her away. He had written to tell her when he was persuaded to sell the house but her spidery handwriting had never, in response, been waiting among the day's brown envelopes on the floor of the hall.

It wasn't again this morning. The estate agents wrote to say appointments had been made for would-be purchasers: today at half past two, at four o'clock, at five. *We are delighted with this brisk response*, the communication ended, *and are confident of an offer soon*.

After breakfast he brought to life the embers of his bonfire, throwing on to them more photographs he had found, his plaintive school reports, his father's diaries, and magazines and packs of cards. He watched the photographs becoming wisps of black that floated off to decorate eleagnus and mahonia. He scattered over a blaze of chairs with broken backs or missing legs the postcards of Italian art his mother had collected – five shoeboxes of masterworks in black and white, each with a greeting in a different hand, all of them stamped and franked, job lots found somewhere. When a few fell at his feet he threw them on to the fire and later discovered one where it had dropped, unnoticed, on the grass a few yards away. A monk prayed to a saint who had been stabbed, the dagger that pierced her throat still there. The wound was bloodless, the sacred features unaffected by the ordeal. 'Santa Lucia,' he read, and told himself it was imagination that he was reminded of the girl he had talked to in Rathmoye.

8

Days passed, and then a week. A warm June gave way to July heat. Already the land was parched, grass lost its green. Dust gathered in Rathmoye's streets, litter lay in gutters unwashed by rain.

On a Wednesday morning when the new month was not far advanced, Joseph Paul Connulty walked through the town with a bunch of dahlias and asparagus fern. Since his mother's death he had done so once a week, his intention being that what he placed on her grave should never be seen to droop and wither. Asparagus fern was consistently the green accompaniment, the choice of flowers depending on what was available in Cadogan's Vegetables and Floral.

In the cemetery he changed the water in the glass container and dropped the blooms he had taken from it into a wire waste-bin supplied for this purpose. They would have lasted a few more days, even a week, but since he did not consider it fanciful that his mother each time witnessed the purchase made in Cadogan's and the walk through the town, the changing of the water, the fresh flowers arranged, he did not take chances. It could have been that he had once, when in the cemetery, heard his mother utter – in a murmur no louder than a whisper – an expression of gratitude. But, practical man of business that he was, publican and coal merchant, who paid his debts and charged what he must, he suspected that that had been some errant sound, transformed in his thoughts to seem, momentarily, what it was not: the certainty of his faith and its related beliefs did not ever exceed his own laid-down limits of the likely.

He left the cemetery and returned to his back bar, which was the centre of his business life. In half an hour Bernadette O'Keeffe from the coal office would arrive with cheques for him to sign, with copies of the invoices that had been dispatched for the second or third time and had still failed to elicit a response, with anything of importance that might have come in the morning post. All bills relating to the running of the bed-and-breakfast accommodation at Number 4 The Square were recorded in the office books and settled as soon as they came in. Once a week, on Friday evenings, Joseph Paul removed a sum from the till, its total agreed upon with his mother in her lifetime and paid now to his sister. The notes and loose change were laid out by him on the kitchen windowsill as they always had been.

A fly crept about on the ceiling and idly he watched it while he waited. He had never killed a fly; it wasn't something he could do. He poured himself a glass of 7-Up, which he found invigorating at this time of day. He continued his observation of the rambling fly as it went about whatever task it had set itself.

*

That morning Bernadette O'Keeffe was delayed. She was a few minutes late leaving the coal yards and was then importuned by Orpen Wren, who was waiting for her in the doorway of Kissane the jeweller's.

'What coal are we talking about, Mr Wren?' she enquired, knowing they were talking about nothing.

'It's the same order as ever it is. Would the winter stocks be in the yards yet?'

'It's only July, Mr Wren.'

'September they light the fires.'

'Who's that, then?' Bernadette asked, knowing the answer to this question too.

'George Anthony's come back. Lisquin's opened up like you'd remember it. Well, you'd know George Anthony's back.'

'I'm afraid I didn't.'

'Put them down for coal.'

'I will of course, Mr Wren.'

Stylish, blonded, in her two-piece of flecked cherry-red, Bernadette passed on. She was forty-six, younger than her employer, younger than his sister, who was imperious when they met, which was too often for Bernadette. The imperiousness was the mother's, although the daughter did not know it or she would have changed her ways. Her employer's sister was a sinister woman in Bernadette's opinion.

She passed into the public house and through the long street bar, no one at present in charge of it. There were drinkers at the far end, two men who were always there in the mornings, who never greeted her when she came in, or spoke to her when she passed close to them, whose names she did not know or wish to know.

'Good morning,' she said in the back bar, and her employer rose from the small round table where they did their business and she sat down at it. He poured her a 7-Up.

They were alone. There never was anyone else in the back bar when she came, or even later in the day; and in the evenings the street bar was still preferred. At that time the priests frequented the back bar, and Mr McGovern because it was convenient, and Fogarty from the court-house to play cards if there was anyone to play with.

Bernadette spread out the papers she had brought, the cheques to be signed kept to one side. For a long time this had been a morning routine, the 7-Up, and watching while the top of her employer's ballpoint was removed, his signature inscribed. This declaration of his identity was as meticulous and tidy as he was himself, a man who respected restraint, who never raised his voice or displayed anger, who lost nothing because he would not let himself lose things. Bernadette loved him.

'We're low on Hennessy,' he said.

'I'll give them a ring.'

She didn't have to make a note; she never forgot. He said Father Millane had been in last evening. An awkwardness had arisen in connection with the garden of remembrance: an old right-of-way over the piece of ground that had been earmarked was going to make its purchase troublesome.

'I think I heard,' she said.

'Father Millane is set on stained glass instead. Seemingly, he has always had an Annunciation in mind for the three empty windows in the north wall.'

'How's Miss Connulty on that, though?'

'She isn't keen.'

'An Annunciation would be lovely.'

'There's a place in the cemetery fence where Magourtey's

bullocks get in. My sister is saying we could improve the fence.'

'In memory of your mother, is it?'

'My sister has a wild way of talking.'

'Still and all, a fence isn't much. A wire fence, is it? I don't think I ever noticed it.'

'Wire on concrete posts.'

'Your mother was practical in her ways. Miss Connulty is thinking of that.'

'Oh, you can't have bullocks hammering away at people's graves, no doubt about that at all. There'll be a job done on the fence as a matter of course. But seemingly the bishop would like to see the north wall given significance, too. So Father Millane'll be speaking to her.'

Bernadette agreed that a few words from the priest would be the way to go about it.

'The latest thing she's got into her head,' Joseph Paul said, 'is that a fellow was taking photographs at the funeral.'

Bernadette, who had observed the taking of the photographs and had heard this spoken about with disapproval afterwards, who had been informed that the same man had been to the coal yards in her absence, that he'd been given the keys of the Coliseum in order to take further photographs, nevertheless agreed that Miss Connulty imagined things. She watched her employer reading through a reference offered by a man who had applied for work in the yards, a communication that had come this morning. He nodded, satisfied, as he folded it into its envelope. He asked her to write and thank whoever it was who had communicated so helpfully.

'No, I've done that,' she said, and found what she had written for him to sign. He shifted slightly on his chair while he reached for it and for a moment Bernadette was aware of the edge of a trouser turn-up on the calf of her leg and knew that it was accidentally there.

'Well, we're all in order,' her employer said, which was how he always concluded their morning sessions.

*

When he had again spoken to Bernadette O'Keeffe, on her way back to the coal yards, Orpen Wren remained for a little longer in Kissane's doorway before going to the post office, where he made enquiries about George Anthony St John, whether or not he had been in since his return. The woman there shook her head and Orpen made similar enquiries at the barber's in Cashel Street and Mac's Hairdressing in Irish Street. He asked in McGovern's. Then he sat in the Square.

He spread the papers he always carried on the seat beside him, smoothed them, and read their contents. For all the years of his travels he had daily read what was written there, had nodded his agreement and been reassured by his own divinations. Resting this morning, he was reassured again.

George Anthony would be occupied at Lisquin. He naturally would be. All the family would be; you couldn't expect different. There'd be rooks in the chimneys, the windows stuck, the locks gone rusty. It would take more than a month, more than two, even three, to get a big house going again, and all you could do was to have the papers ready. Sooner or later, when the air was fresher in the rooms and any window bars had been replaced where

71

they'd become unsafe, when the chimneys had been swept and painters brought in, the busy time would come to an end and George Anthony would have a moment to accept the papers and return them to the drawer where they belonged. Sooner or later he would be in the town again with business to do – advice to get from a solicitor, or to have a tooth extracted, or have his hair cut. He'd maybe have to be measured for a suit of clothes; or there'd be valuables to take out of safe-keeping, provisions to order. It wasn't a hardship for Orpen Wren to wait.

9

Later that same day Miss Connulty prepared beef for a stew, cutting it into oblong pieces, dusting them with flour when she had teased out what fat and sinew she could, then laying them ready on a dinner-plate while she diced carrots and onions. She seared and browned the meat, turning the pieces over once and then sliding them into the saucepan in which the vegetables were. She poured on boiling water, added salt and Bisto and put the lid on. She scrubbed her chopping-board, washed bowls and knives in the sink. The saucepan lid rattled; she turned the heat down.

It was half past four. The meat would be tender, or tender enough, by seven, which was when an evening meal was served, the house being back to normal after the death. A change was that Miss Connulty now took her own meals with the daily girl in the kitchen, and gave her brother his either alone or with the overnight lodgers in the dining-room. Before that, a table had always been laid for three in what her mother had called the family room, adjoining the kitchen and so cramped and small you could hardly get round the table with the dishes. It would be used as a store now, and already tins were stacked on the mantelpiece and on the table itself. It was a much more sensible arrangement, which Miss Connulty had repeatedly suggested and had each time been ignored.

She set out plates and dishes ready for the oven later. She mixed mustard and filled the salt cellars. Gohery was still away on his summer holidays. The Clover Meats traveller was due, and the Drummond's Seeds man. She doubted there'd be anyone else. She counted knives and forks and put them ready, with a jug of water and glasses. She left the kitchen then and made her way upstairs, as every afternoon at this time she did, to the bedroom that now was hers, the largest, airiest room in the house, catching the best of the morning sun.

She dabbed on eau-de-Cologne in case the onions lingered on her clothes; reflected in the dressing-table looking-glass, she settled pins into her hair and applied a little powder to her nose and cheeks. A few days after the death she had moved into this room – out of the smaller one where she'd been visited by Arthur Tetlow. Traveller in veterinary requirements, trapped in a marriage in Sheffield, Arthur Tetlow had gone to fight in the war that was already threatening when he'd stayed in the house for the last time. She knew he had, and when peace eventually came there had been the hope that he would once more drive into the Square as so often he had, in the same green English-registered Ford, its celluloid rear window repaired with tape; that he would look up and see her, and hurry to the house. But instead Arthur Tetlow had disappeared into the war, taking with him the promises he had made in good faith and the future they had talked about. No man could help being caught up in a war.

Honouring that time, Miss Connulty lifted her choice for today from the cushion of a tiny velvet-clad box: the sapphire earrings. She took a sleeper from each ear and replaced them with the glittering blue clusters. A ceremony her afternoon adorning of herself had become this summer, the occasion each time finished with another dab of eau-de-Cologne, another touch of lip salve. She stayed a little longer when she'd completed all that, contemplating without emotion her reflected image in the looking-glass. Then she settled everything back where it belonged on the dressing-table, the jewellery in the shallow top drawer.

On the way downstairs she stood looking out into the Square from the window he would have seen her at if he had come back instead of having to fight for his country. 'Talk sense,' her mother had ridiculed all that: back to some strumpet of a wife was where he'd gone; a man like that would only have a strumpet for a wife.

Her mother had burnt the sheets, tearing them from the bed, ordering the daily woman out of the house to sweep the yard, then carrying the sheets downstairs and poking them into the range. Her mother had poured scorn on tears and pleading, on the trust placed in Arthur Tetlow's promises, on his talk about Sheffield and coming back. All of it was pathetic, her mother said: the pair of them would be punished for their craven appetites; both of them would suffer all their lives. The ugly misfortune that had fallen upon the family would always be there, her mother predicted, a consequence that was ugly too.

'Your daughter's a hooer,' her greeting was when her husband came in from the back bar of the public house, the smell of burning sheets still in the air. And when he heard what he had to hear he vowed he would go to Sheffield after Arthur Tetlow and kill him stone dead.

But instead he took his daughter on the bus to Dublin and held her hand the whole time, through Roscrea and Monasterevin and over the Curragh, and when the bus drew up in Naas she had to get off because she was feeling sick. A man came up to him on O'Connell Bridge and asked him how was he and he said grand, although he wasn't. He gave the man a coin, because it was always his way to give beggars something. He told her to pray as soon as she lay down, before they'd do anything to her.

It was a chemist's shop he took her to and they closed it before they began. They turned the notice round on the door and pulled the blind down over the glass. They told her father to wait there and he said to her when she came out from the back that they'd have a cup of tea and they had it in the tea lounge of the Adelphi cinema. He got a car to drive them back to the quays and they went on the bus again. Her mother said he was a murderer when they got back, maybe half past ten it was. A bed had been made up for him in an attic and he slept there that night and always afterwards. Nothing more was ever said between her mother and her father.

The events of that day had not receded for Miss Connulty. Her cruelty to the dead was their ceremonial preservation: the time for pain was over, yet her wish was that it should not be, that there should always be something left – a wince, a tremor, some part of her anger that was not satisfied.

10

They asked the same questions. They enquired about the drains, they trudged around the attics. They asked if the soil was alkaline, they wondered about the electric wiring, they noticed ill-fitting windows. A few were alarmed by the water rats. Others turned around and drove away.

Florian had propped up on one of the kitchen windowsills the postcard he hadn't thrown on to his bonfire. By the lesser Ghirlandaio the painting was, the card's recipient Miss Mabel Thynne of 21 The Paddocks, Cheltenham. *Weather heavenly*, a message read, *this city too*. Reduced to sepia tints, the innocence Ghirlandaio had painted was not entirely lost, and the resemblance Florian had told himself was imagination he noticed still. Bored by people expressing surprise at the reduced condition of the drawing-room and asking questions he was unable to answer, he returned one morning to Rathmoye.

*

'I have them for you,' Mr Clancy said, a wiry, bustling man who liked to keep a conversation going. 'Wait now till I'll see.'

All the boots and shoes that were ready – soled or heeled or both, new laces put in, polished – were on a shelf above the muddle of work yet to be done. None was labelled, nor was there a note on any of what was owing. Mr Clancy always knew.

'Is himself in form?' he enquired, finding Dillahan's black Sunday shoes, new heels on both.

'He's all right,' Ellie said.

'And yourself, Mrs Dillahan?'

'I'm all right.'

They waited for her to be pregnant. In the shops, at the presbytery, old Mrs Connulty in her lifetime, her daughter now. Miss Burke at the wool counter often glanced to see. A few had given up, as Ellie had herself.

She paid for the repairs. Those shoes were worn so little they would see him out, Mr Clancy predicted. A shoe wasn't made like that any more, he added, shining each one of the pair before he put both on the counter.

'Wait a minute while I'll get you change,' he said.

But he didn't have it and Ellie went away with her ten-shilling note to try the Matthew Street shops.

*

Without knowing how it had got there, Florian looked down at the tidy sheaf of documents that was already in his hands. *Her Majesty's Sloop* The Serpent *being designed for a Foreign Voyage*, he read, *you are, by the Board's direction, to Supply her with additional Ordnance Stores proper for the same.*

'That's very interesting,' he said.

He had been taken unawares by the diminutive presence beside him on the street. 'I've cared for them this long while,' Orpen Wren was saying. 'They've accompanied me for many a year.'

Florian attempted to return the papers, but the old

librarian was reluctant to receive them, and said again that he had cared for them. It was the third George in the family who'd been a naval man, he said.

'But you'd know, of course, sir.'

Florian didn't deny that, since there seemed little point in doing so.

'He was two years in the Ordnance Stores, sir, and longer before he got his command. The St Johns never set themselves up in a naval way.'

'Of course not.'

'I mentioned in McGovern's a while back you'd be in for supplies, sir. I took a liberty with that. You'll find them expecting you in McGovern's, sir.'

'Yes.'

'The family always insisted on McGovern's.'

'Yes, of course.'

Florian gazed into the lined, pouched features, the tired eyes, and saw reflected there a hesitation, a moment of doubt, bewilderment, before the old man again found his way in the conversation.

'I have the coal ordered,' he said.

'Of course, but all the same it might be better if you went on looking after these papers yourself.'

'The little table beneath the portrait of Lady Eliza is where the papers were always kept. The little table that opens out. Well, you'd know.'

'Just for the time-being, maybe you wouldn't mind continuing to look after them?'

'We've had the time-being, sir. The longest time-being there ever was known in Ireland.'

Florian saw the girl then. She was cycling slowly across

the Square in the distance. Her blue dress drew his attention, the same dress she'd been wearing before and when he dreamed about her. She passed Bodell's Bar and turned into a street a few yards on.

'If you wouldn't mind,' he said, 'another day would be more convenient for me to take the papers.'

They were accepted then, when again Florian held them out.

'I've lent them a few times, sir, because of the interest in the family. But I'll keep them by me since it's your instruction. Where I live these days is Morpeth Terrace, the second house along. It does me rightly.'

Florian nodded. In the drawer of that same table, he was reminded, was the catalogue of the library, complete and clearly written out, two thousand and fifty-nine volumes. In case it should ever be mislaid there was a copy in the smaller of the two upstairs drawing-rooms, in the Limerick writing-desk.

'Mr Macready himself delivered that desk, sir, and said keep it a distance from the fire-grate. That same time he said he could put secret drawers in the shutters if that would be convenient, but the governess wouldn't have them. It was a schoolroom, the small drawing-room, temporary when William's leg went. Miss Batesriff that governess was.'

'I have to be off now, I'm afraid.'

'It's the best thing ever happened in Ireland, sir, yourself come back.'

*

Ellie put the change she'd been given on the counter. Mr Clancy divided it.

'Tell your husband I was asking for him, Mrs Dillahan,'

he requested. 'Not that I ever knew him personally. It was his mother brought in his boots, then again his wife. And these days it's yourself.'

'I'll tell him, Mr Clancy.'

The bell above the door sounded as she left.

'Hullo,' a voice said on the street.

She knew before she turned round to look. She had the shoes, unwrapped, still in her hand, about to put them into the basket of her bicycle.

'Florian Kilderry,' he said. 'D'you remember?'

He was standing in front of the window of the closed premises next door to the shoemaker's, his bicycle beside him. He was wearing a hat. He smiled at her. 'You've forgotten me,' he said.

She felt the colour mounting in her face, as it had before. Her thoughts became disordered, as they had become then too, perverse and separated from her, as if they were not hers. She wanted to say that of course she remembered him. She wanted to say that she had wondered about him, that she had tried not to, that she had known she should not. She wanted to say she had known immediately who it was when he'd said hullo.

'A cup of coffee?' he suggested.

'No.' She said it more sharply than she'd intended. She shook her head.

'I thought you might like a cup of coffee.'

He wheeled his bicycle beside hers when she moved on. 'It's just I thought you might,' he said.

In the silence that came she tried to say she hadn't meant to sound severe. But she didn't say that either.

'I live near Castledrummond,' he said. 'My father died

a while ago and I got left with a house a few miles out.'

'I heard of Castledrummond.'

'D'you like Rathmoye, Ellie?'

'You get to know a place.'

'Not much goes on, I imagine.'

'There's a Strawberry Fair and people come in for that.'

He had a way of looking at the ground while they were walking as if he'd lost something. Once he stopped to pick something up, but threw it away again.

'An old man I meet on the streets thinks I'm someone else,' he said.

'That'd be Orpen Wren. He'd talk to you about Lisquin, would he?'

'What's Lisquin?'

'The St Johns were there one time. They're gone from it years ago.'

'I think Mr Wren is under the impression that I'm one of them come back.'

'Lisquin isn't there any more.'

Only the back gate-lodge was left, she said, tumbled down, on the old Kilaney road. She said she went there now and again to cut the lavender.

They were in the poor part of the town. Slums had been cleared, the shoemaker's the last small shop doing business. They had let him stay where he was, Mr Clancy had told Ellie once; they would allow him to until he was too old to trade. She said that now, explaining all the boarded windows.

'You don't live near here, Ellie?'

'I'm on a farm out at Cnocrea. In the Crilly hills.'

Nothing about him was different. She couldn't prevent

herself from looking at him and once he saw. When he did he smiled at her and she wondered if he knew she had feelings for him. She didn't want him to know.

'There'd be butterflies if there's lavender,' he said.

'Oh, there are butterflies all right.'

'Where did the St Johns go?'

'Away from Ireland altogether. I don't know why they would have.'

'The old man was a servant, was he?'

'I don't know is it right, only people say he had charge of a library there.'

'I think maybe it is right.'

He reached out with his foot and kicked a bottle-top off the edge of the pavement into the gutter. It frightened her almost that they were walking together with their bicycles, not even going in the right direction for Hearn's, where she had meat to get. She should have said she had shopping to do. She should say it now that she had the meat to get, only she didn't.

'Mr Wren has papers he wants me to take from him.'

'He always has the papers.'

He offered her a cigarette, holding out the packet, the silver paper folded back. She shook her head.

'Don't you ever smoke?'

'I never did.'

He picked a coin up from the pavement.

'Worth nothing,' he said, handing it to her. 'The kind that was minted by a business in the old days.'

Boyce, she read on it, and he said that would be a shop-keeper's name. 'Boyces were Wexford people,' he said.

She'd say she had to go into Corbally's when they came

to Magennis Street: she had that ready, even to mention what she had to get. Press-studs she'd say, needles.

'I'm alone in the house I got left with,' he said. 'Myself and a black dog.'

*

Florian expected no more of this morning than he had of other casual relationships brought about in the same manner and for the same reason. This beginning was as previous beginnings had been, its distraction potent enough already. Isabella would never be just a shadow, but this morning an artless country girl had stirred a tenderness in him and already his cousin's voice echoed less confidently, her smile was perhaps a little blurred, her touch less than yesterday's memory of it. He might, in making conversation, have remarked upon his present companion's attractions, but he sensed it was better not to, maybe not ever.

'Shelhanagh the house is called,' he said instead, and Ellie asked about the dog and he told her, and about the lake, and the garden in the evening, which was when he liked it best. He had never lived anywhere else, he said. He'd never wanted to; nor had his mother or his father since they had come to live in Ireland. His mother had been Italian, he said.

'When she died, the life went out of my father too. Although he managed. He was always good at managing.'

'Were you born in that house?'

'Yes, I was. I was a surprise for them. They'd given up, since they were getting on a bit.'

'Is it big, the house?'

'Eighteen dilapidated rooms.'

*

Ellie saw them, without dilapidation: comfortable rooms with fires and flowers, two people who were his mother and father, the child who'd come as a surprise. She saw him alone there now, his black dog, the eighteen rooms too many since the deaths. There was the still water of a lake. There were a garden's scents and its delicious twilight air.

The coin he'd picked up was in her hand, pressed into her palm by the rubber grip on the handlebars. She had never seen a coin the same as it before and she knew she wanted to keep it and that she would.

In Hurley Lane they wheeled their bicycles around children playing hopscotch. His cigarette was still unlit between his fingers, as if he had forgotten it; but he hadn't because he stopped to light it now.

*

Striking a match, Florian remembered watching her making room in her basket for the shoes. It might have crossed his mind, scarcely there at all, that they'd be her father's, or a brother's, that probably she had several brothers; he couldn't remember. He hadn't noticed the ring he saw when he looked for it now – so skimpy, so unemphatic on her finger it could have come out of a Hallowe'en barm brack.

'I didn't know,' he said, gesturing at it.

'I'm married this good while,' she said.

*

They passed Corbally's. She wondered if, hardly knowing what she did, she had kept her ring out of sight when they were in the Cash and Carry, if she'd kept it out of sight this morning too. Be careful what you'd do not knowing you were doing it, the nuns would say: no matter what, it was yourself doing it.

They reached the Square and they stood there, not saying anything. People could see them, she didn't care.

'I might go looking for your tumbled-down gate-lodge one of these days,' he said. 'Since it's all that's left of what I've been hearing so much about from the old man. I might do that.'

'Three miles out on the old Kilaney road. It's easy enough to find.'

'I dreamed about you,' he said.

Resting after her morning's work, idling at the window from which so often she viewed the Square, Miss Connulty had noticed the two when they appeared there from Magennis Street. She had seen them hesitating before walking on, seen them stop again, seen Ellie Dillahan eventually scuttling off. Miss Connulty used that word to herself, for scuttling was what Ellie Dillahan's abrupt breaking away had looked like, a sudden, awkward movement forced upon herself, reluctant yet urgent. She hadn't mounted her bicycle but had dragged it with her, and the man who'd taken the photographs at the funeral stood where she had left him, taken aback by her hasty departure. Then he rode across the Square and disappeared on to the Castledrummond road.

There had been something about how they were with one another, something Miss Connulty might not even have noticed – and certainly would not have considered significant – had Ellie Dillahan been a stranger to her. Clearly, the two knew one another better than they had at the time Ellie Dillahan had spoken of, when he had asked her for directions.

A car with a caravan attached was attempting to reverse and finding it difficult. One of Joseph Paul's lorries, loaded with turf, passed into Matthew Street. What she had witnessed bewildered Miss Connulty, and now appalled her.

Ellie Dillahan was a girl it was impossible not to feel protective of because of what her life had been. Her husband was a decent man, respected and sober, and it was understandable that he hadn't been comfortable in himself since the tragedy he had suffered. But maybe it was no joke for Ellie to be out there in the hills, to have the days passing and not a word exchanged except with a husband who couldn't forgive himself for an error. It wasn't easy to blame Ellie; you wouldn't want to and it didn't seem natural to do so. Child of an institution, child of need and of humility, born into nothing, expecting nothing, Ellie Dillahan was victim enough without the attentions of a suave photographer. No matter who he was or where he came from, in Miss Connulty's bristling imagination he was already a plunderer. Still watching the reversing of the caravan, she kept that with her, her outrage becoming an anger that brought two bright flushes to her cheeks.

The house was silent, the daily girl gone home early since today was the day for that. Miss Connulty remained at the window for a minute or so longer, then went downstairs to make her brother's lunchtime sandwiches. Her fury had quietened but still was there, as the dead days of finished time were, and tears no longer shed. She felt a wave of pity for Ellie Dillahan, as once, so wretchedly, she had for herself.

*

It was unusual for his sister to sit down opposite him in the dining-room when she brought his sandwiches and the strong cup of Bovril Joseph Paul liked to have with them. She had something to say and he knew she had, but

88

when she spoke he didn't listen. Instead, from time to time he nodded.

The day their father had taken her to Dublin, their mother had said she hoped they would never come back. Neither of them, she said, not ever. But he had wanted them to come back; no matter how horrible the shame, he had wanted them to be on the evening bus, or on tomorrow's bus, to come back some time. Waiting, not knowing, the notice in the downstairs window stating that the house was full when it wasn't, he had thought his mother would cry, but she didn't; he'd never seen her cry. In the afternoon he brought her tea and made her toast. She couldn't eat it, and later on she didn't hear him when he asked her would he go down the town to see if they were on the bus. She said she knew they would be when he asked her again; when they came back to the house with him she said it was the worst day of her life. He brought his sister cocoa. Any mother would be upset, he said, but his sister didn't answer, the first time she ever didn't when he spoke to her. Quite often now they didn't answer one another.

'He made enquiries from Ellie Dillahan about the picture house,' she said in the dining-room, and he asked her what she was talking about.

'I told you.'

'I know, I know. But it isn't easy to get at the gist of what you're saying.'

'He's hanging about the town. He got into the picture house – I've had that said to me. There's nobody knows who he is.'

'The keys of the picture house are in the yard office.

There's no way you can get into the picture house except you have the keys. I don't know this man you're talking about.'

'A pale tweed suit and he's taken to wearing a hat. He comes in off the Castledrummond road.'

'I don't know him at all.'

His lack of interest spread into Joseph Paul's tone. No one should be listening to this, he said to himself, and aloud said that Bernadette O'Keeffe was making arrangements with Dempsey to have the back bedrooms repainted.

'The back bedrooms have nothing to do with it. There's no one but yourself hasn't seen him. He could be shouting from the rooftops and you wouldn't see him.'

He said nothing. It was always best to say nothing. He finished the sandwiches she had made for him, and the dregs of the Bovril. He waited for her to go away.

*

She took the tray from where she'd left it on the dumb waiter. She put his plate and his cup and saucer on it, with the salt and pepper she always brought him too. She cleared up the crumbs he'd made, brushing them with a dish-cloth on to the tray.

'I'll tell you another thing,' she said, as calm as ice, which she could be at will.

She spoke to his back; he didn't turn his head. Before he was finished with her, this man would be off with Ellie Dillahan, she said, and then she went away.

12

Ellie held the tyre lever in place; he'd shown her how. For five or six inches the tyre had been released from the wheel's rim and two other levers were holding it there. He worked one of them with his foot, coaxing the tyre, and when he wasn't successful sliding the other closer to the one she still held. Further inches of the tyre's grip were released. 'We have it now,' he said.

He ran the lever along, then pulled the tube out. He had jacked the Vauxhall up and taken the wheel off without her help, calling her only a few minutes ago. He'd filled a basin with water. She watched while he pumped the tube up and found the puncture. 'I'll manage now,' he said.

In the crab-apple orchard she scattered grain and the hens came rushing to her. She hadn't been aware that she didn't love her husband. Love hadn't come into it, had never begun in a way that was different from the love spoken of so often by the nuns at Cloonhill, its brightly visible sign burning perpetually, as it did above the kitchen doorway in the farmhouse, as it had for the woman who once had scoured the saucepans that now were hers, and for other women before that. She closed the hens in and cut two lettuces on her way back to the yard. She picked the best of the chives.

The wheel had been replaced, the jack wound down.

'Thanks for that,' her husband said as she went by. He had that way with him, of thanking her.

It was a kindness – so it had seemed to her, and still did – when she had been offered marriage; it would have been unkind on her part if she'd said no. Her home was his house, where in kindness, too, she had been called his housekeeper, not a maid. She thought of him, even now, as older than he was, being widowed and knowing more than she did. It would be better if they were married: he hadn't put it like that, and afterwards, at Lahinch, had said he'd grown close to her and was a lucky man. 'I'm lucky myself,' she'd said, and had meant it, for she had never developed the habit of lying. 'I'm sorry,' she apologized later when she couldn't give him children, and he said it didn't matter. 'You've given me enough,' he said.

She laid the table. She washed the lettuce and dried it in a tea-towel. She sliced what remained of the lamb they'd had on Sunday. She chopped the chives, cut up tomatoes.

He took his wellingtons off at the door; he washed his hands at the sink. Sometimes he washed upstairs and changed his shirt, but he didn't this evening. She could tell he was tired.

'A bit of a blade,' he said, explaining the puncture. 'Vicious little edge to it.'

Another day had passed, the fifth that had since the encounter outside the shoemaker's. Nothing was less than it had been; she had imagined that by now it would be. She was contrite, and ashamed, but still her feelings were as they'd been that morning and before it.

'I see we have the raddle powder.' He piled salad on to

his plate. Summer fare, he called it, and never minded when it was there again.

'I forgot to say it came in.'

'No harm. Did you ever notice hook springs in English's? D'you know do they keep them?'

'I'll ask.'

She poured out tea for him, and added milk. She pushed the sugar closer to him. She tried to think of something else to say because talking was a help. 'He'd do anything for you,' a woman she didn't know had said to her at the wedding celebration, as if that should be said, as if it was too easy to take him for granted. The de Valera man in McGovern's had terrier pups for sale again, she said.

'I think you maybe told me that.'

'I'm sorry.'

'Arrah, no.'

The woman at the wedding had called her fortunate. Afterwards, when they'd driven off in the Vauxhall, she hadn't been unhappy. She hadn't had regrets, either then or in the few days they spent away. She hadn't when they returned to the farm. In Rathmoye when people called her Mrs Dillahan it pleased her. Only that, and sharing his bedroom with him, had been different. The little room where she'd slept before would have been the child's, brightly painted, a wallpaper with toys on it. She had never liked to change it and when it was empty he'd said to leave it as it was and she knew what he was thinking.

He stirred sugar into the tea she'd poured. A silence didn't matter; he never minded that, he'd often said it.

'We cut the road pasture,' he said when he had finished what was on his plate. 'I had Corrigan's lads over.'

She watched him removing the silver paper from a tri-angle of cheese, tidily turning back the folds, then lifting the cheese out on his knife. He liked to do things well, even that. It was impossible to imagine him careless, or casual. And yet, of course, tragically he had been.

'You're off your food, Ellie,' he said.

'A bit.'

'I noticed.'

She cut more bread for him, and reached across the table to fill his cup again. Gahagan was getting closer to letting the field go, he said.

'Contrary as he is, he's nearly ready to part with it.'

She tried to think about the field changing hands and the difference it would make, and Gahagan maybe consid-ering the disposal of the woodlands too.

'We'll mark that day, Ellie.'

He nodded each word into place as he spoke, then pushed his chair back. When he was tired in the evenings he sat on the sagging couch in the window, his big shoulders relaxed over the paper, the radio on if it was something he wanted. He sat there now, and Ellie cleared the table and carried the dishes to the sink. At first there'd been a photograph of his wife in the other room, a smiling woman, the infant in her arms. But later he had put it in a drawer.

She ran the hot tap over plates and cutlery and squeezed washing-up liquid into the water when it covered them. His old-time dancing programme was on the radio. *There's nothing only weakness in me*: she saw her handwriting, old-fashioned, slanting, influenced by the strictures of Sister Ambrose, who had emphasized the virtues of clarity over flamboyance. 'Always write to us if you'd need us,' Sister Ambrose had begged. 'Always tell us.' God is your strength: how often a nun's lips had expressed that!

More days would pass, and one would come when it would seem as though what had happened hardly had. She would shamefully recount her errors, her deception even of herself, and make her peace and be forgiven through contrition. Time could not but pass, every minute of it a healing.

'I used go to old-time myself,' her husband said, and she guessed he'd gone with his other wife and hadn't wanted to since because of what had happened. He said something else, drumming his fingers on the arm of the couch. But the music was suddenly too loud and she didn't hear what it was.

'I'd better see to the fowls.'

One of the dogs had barked and there'd been a fox about. But when she went out everything was quiet. It was never dark at this time of year: the green of the tractor hadn't faded, or the dusty brown of the Vauxhall. The sheepdogs went with her when she made her rounds, and stood beside her, obedient in the gateway when she listened there. His Italian mother would have smoked cigarettes, a tall, still beautiful woman: out of nowhere that image came. In the crab-apple orchard she locked her hens in.

'Sit down and rest yourself,' her husband said. 'Sit down and listen to this.'

'I've the accounts to look at, though.'

She went to the other room. The receipts were there and the record she kept in a grey exercise book of cheques that had been paid in at the bank. She turned the light on and took the exercise book from the drawer of the table in the window.

The accounts were up to date: she'd known they would be. But in the same drawer were the Christmas cards she had received from Sister Ambrose, who had been, more than the other nuns, her friend at Cloonhill. *We are delighted*, a note recorded in one, *that you are to marry and we give thanks for your contentment on the farm*. In another there was news of a journey to Lough Derg, and of the Fermoy Retreat. 'We are here for you if ever you feel called to join us,' she remembered Sister Ambrose saying on the evening of the day that had been chosen as her birthday. 'And never forget that we are here for you in other ways too.' She was eleven then.

She returned the cards to their envelopes. A few had come with a sacred text, a shiny slip that illustrated a moment from Christ's Passion. *Our sins are His wounds*, hard black italic type declared, beneath the bleeding figure. *His agony was for us*.

She heard her husband's footsteps on the stairs, his movements in the room above. She tore a single sheet from the exercise book and took from the drawer the ballpoint pen she always kept there. She wrote to Sister Ambrose, saying she was sorry she hadn't written at Christmas, saying she was all right. But even so she asked for Sister Ambrose's prayers. She wrote what she had written in her thoughts and the words did not make sense. Looking at them, she knew they would not unless she revealed why they'd been written, unless she confessed that the nuns, who knew her so well, would not know her now, made different by lies of silence and of deception, and being ashamed. On another page, when she tried again there were no other words, no other way of conveying, while telling too little, the bleakness she felt. And even too little would bewilder and alarm.

In the silence of the room she sat for another hour, and then for longer. She did not weep, although she wanted to. The sympathy she sought was there, she knew it was; yet she resisted it.

She unbolted the back door and went outside again. She walked on the road, the night air refreshing, a relief. She walked to tire herself, the sheepdogs going with her. In the kitchen when she returned she opened the stove and dropped the pages she had torn from the exercise book on to black, unglowing anthracite. She pulled the dampers out and listened to the flame beginning.

13

Miss Connulty said he was bad news. Taking in the eggs she said it, not looking at Ellie. People were wondering who he was, she said, fiddling with the money she was counting from her purse. Miss Connulty knew.

More change was added to the coins, the purse zipped up.

'You didn't mind me mentioning that?' Miss Connulty said.

'I only know him on account of he asked me the way that day.'

He wasn't bad news. Riding away, Ellie told herself she should have said he wasn't. How could you call a person bad news when you didn't know who he was or anything about him? She should have said that too. 'His name is Florian Kilderry,' she should have said. 'He's half Italian.'

She went back to the farm the long way, by the old Kilaney road. She had ignored it when he'd shown an interest in the Lisquin gate-lodge. She hadn't said she liked the quietness there, that she went there more often than she had implied. She wondered if he had sensed that suppression and been hurt by it, and again been hurt when she'd been abrupt, not saying goodbye. Would it have mattered much going to Meagher's Café with him? Hearing him called bad news made a difference. And how could nuns understand? How could they? And was there harm in talking to a person when nothing wrong was said?

On the old Kilaney road, used by no one these days, she thought she smelt the cigarettes he smoked. She stopped for a moment, but she was wrong. Going slowly, she passed the high iron gates of the Lisquin avenue, and glanced in at the tumbled-down gate-lodge. No one was there.

*

'I'm going up the hills,' Dillahan said. 'There's a couple out.'

Ellie didn't answer, as if she hadn't heard.

'You'd tell me, Ellie? You'd tell me if you were troubled?'

She said she was all right. 'Really,' she said.

He drove out of the yard. Gahagan had told him about the sheep that were wandering. Gahagan went up there sometimes although he didn't have any stock there. He'd seen two blue-marked sheep, he'd said, not that he was sure of it, his eyes the way they were. But if he didn't go and look for himself, Dillahan predicted, it would turn out that the two were his.

He went a different way from usual, turning off to the right at the Corrigans' black shed. He skirted Doole, and then ascended, the Vauxhall feeling as if it was only just able for the incline. If his sheep were out they would have broken through on this side of Crilly.

The dogs dozed beside him. The air his wound-down window allowed in was fresh and almost chilly. There was something, he thought. Maybe no more than a mood, but a mood wasn't like her, never had been. Breakfast again, she'd hardly touched her food.

He drew the car in to where there was a gap and walked

on, over the boglands. He saw the two white specks and could tell from where they were that they were his. He sent the dogs and went himself to find the break in the wire, his boots sinking into the water surface. She was often shy about something that was a woman's thing and he never pressed her because it wasn't his way to. She wasn't evasive; all the years she'd been in the house she never had been. She hadn't known about a farm when she'd first come and she hadn't pretended she did. He hadn't expected her to know, but she was more skilled than he was now at what she'd become good at – the hens, the dairy, the vegetables she grew, keeping their accounts in order. He had never been inclined to compare her with his first wife; he'd never wanted to think of them together, and never had. But he knew he had been fortunate twice.

He passed near his turf bog and realized there wasn't much of it left. But there was turf that could be cut closer to the boundary of his land, a long strip, wide enough to make working it worthwhile. Over marshy ground, the carting would be difficult, but it could be managed at a dry time. Early next summer he'd decide about that.

Larks flew out of the heather, occasionally a snipe. He found the place where the wire had snapped, and whistled up the dogs. They didn't hurry, knowing not to. He'd thought it was the disappointment of the hens not laying as well as usual. He had asked her if it was that and had watched her forcing herself to smile. She was all right, she'd said then too. It would be nothing, he told himself.

*

She spread the material out on the kitchen table, the paper pattern still pinned to it. She took the pins out and returned the flimsy paper to its folds. The dress was half made, small scarlet rosebuds on a pale ground. She wouldn't finish it today, but perhaps tomorrow.

The sewing-machine had been in the house for as long as her husband could remember, his mother's but passed on to her too. It would have been an extravagance to abandon it for a new one, although Ellie had been offered that. The kitchen table, sturdy on its legs, its surface spacious, was where it had always been used.

She changed the spool and rethreaded the needle, then turned the handle to begin the stitching of her seam. She had known how to sew on a machine when she'd come to the farmhouse; she made her own clothes, could turn a shirt collar and put in a pocket. But she didn't need this dress. She had bought the material and the pattern in Corbally's hardly noticing if she liked either.

Demanding all her attention, which was what she had hoped for, the sewing-machine clattered on. Determinedly, she pushed her seam through, keeping it straight. The afternoon was the worst time. In the morning there were the hens, and Disc of the Day on the radio, a lot of talking between the records. But when it was an afternoon on which Mrs Hadden didn't come, or one when shy little Tomasina Flynn didn't come for the few duck eggs there were, she needed something. She had changed her day for going in to Rathmoye to Tuesday because he knew about Fridays. Tuesday afternoons weren't as convenient as Friday mornings, not for her or for the presbytery, yet she had done it, knowing she should.

She snapped the thread when the seam was finished and reached out for another sleeve. But she didn't feel like continuing now and she sat for a while longer, her sewing-machine silent, her half-made, unwanted dress spread as she had left it. She heard the tractor in the yard and dreaded the long evening.

14

Miss Connulty's overnight lodgers one by one awoke in answer to the clamour of the alarm clock supplied in every room. Each stilled the peremptory summons, stretched and yawned, emerged from the bedclothes, drew back the curtains, then went to check the occupancy or otherwise of the lavatory and the bathroom. Twenty minutes later three men in dark business suits, with collar and tie, and shoes that Miss Connulty had the night before picked up from outside their bedroom doors and polished, descended the stairs to the dining-room. A fourth man, Mr Buckley, was still dressing. Gohery, the metalwork instructor, back now from his summer holidays, was already finishing at the breakfast table. Joseph Paul had not yet returned from early Mass.

'Your eggs?' Miss Connulty called through the hatch she opened between the kitchen and the dining-room when she heard the murmur of voices. 'How'll I do your eggs?'

The men ordered them fried, as usually the preference was. Those of the Horton's traveller were to be turned, which was usual also. All three said yes to Miss Connulty's enquiries as to tomato and sausage. That bacon would be on each plate went without saying. The Wolsey (Ireland) man enquired as to the availability of black pudding this morning and Miss Connulty said there was plenty.

There was a brief delay, during which Gohery rose from

the table. He nodded without speaking to the three men, as he had when each had entered the dining-room. On the stairs he nodded at Mr Buckley, who was making his slow way to the hall, where every morning of his overnight sojourns at Number 4 he had, for close on thirty-five years, tapped the weather-glass that hung beside the hallstand. In the kitchen Miss Connulty heard him greeted and introduced to the man who was a newcomer in the house. She did not need to open the hatch: these days, Mr Buckley took only Weetabix.

The Horton's man enquired as to Mr Buckley's health and was informed that it was first class, which the Horton's man knew was not true: Mr Buckley was a heavily built, drooping man of yellowish pallor and comatose features, whose pretence, to others and to himself, was that he suffered no ailments and was as sprightly as ever he'd been. But it was said in the shops of the towns he visited that he often, these days, made an error in his orders, that alterations were effected by kindly shopkeepers who knew him well and protected him that he might safely reach the retirement he secretly craved, and the pension that went with it. Stationery and fancy goods were his line; in his decline, as in his heyday, he was fondly respected.

The doors of the hatch opened again and a moment later Miss Connulty entered the dining-room with a rack of toast, and buttered bread. She carried from the hatch the plates she had placed there, enquiring from the man who hadn't stayed before if his fried bread was brown enough. He said it was.

'In Rathmoye I wouldn't stop anywhere only here,' the

Horton's man informed him when she'd gone. 'Wouldn't you agree, Mr Buckley?'

Mr Buckley did so and the Wolsey (Ireland) man said you could travel further and fare worse. Tales were exchanged about unfortunate experiences in this respect – damp beds, food that wasn't fit for consumption, problems with drains. He'd never known the bathroom at Number 4 in need of a bar of soap, the Horton's man declared. And heads were nodded when he added that he'd never known the WC without an extra paper roll.

Each man poured tea for himself, passing a metal teapot around the table. Between mouthfuls the Horton's man tapped a cigarette out of a Gold Flake packet and laid it, with matches, on the tablecloth, ready to ignite when his food was consumed. Shirts mainly he took orders for, he confided to the new man; but, in a general way, men's apparel of every description formed his remit. The new man said he was in cement.

In the kitchen the daily girl arrived, no later than she should be. The front door banged, which Miss Connulty knew would be Joseph Paul returning from Mass. He hadn't mentioned the stained-glass windows recently, but she knew that only minutes ago he would have glanced up at the grimy panes which were to be replaced and would have again taken pleasure in Father Millane's proposal of an Annunciation. In time a brass plaque beside it would request prayers for the soul of Eileen Brigid Connulty.

Miss Connulty didn't care any more. They could do what they liked: delicious death had been a richer compensation than she had ever dreamed of. She was in charge, and today she wore the pearls.

'See to the master,' she instructed the daily girl, and went to put her feet up, having been on them since six. She sat in the big front room, the eye of Daniel O'Connell upon her, and she wondered for a moment what he'd been like and came to no conclusion. She dropped off to sleep, although she had not intended to, and was woken by the men returning to their bedrooms, the thump of their footsteps on the stairs, the Horton's man saying you'd feel the better for your breakfast.

At her writing-desk she made out their bills and when she went downstairs left them on the shelf by the front door, more convenient than the hallstand, where in her mother's day they had been left. Each man would pick his up, would rattle the little bell she had moved from the hallstand to the shelf and, hearing the summons, she would answer it.

'Have you spoken to him?' she enquired of her brother in the dining-room, going there when the daily girl had brought in his breakfast.

*

Arranging egg, bacon and a corner of fried bread on his fork, Joseph Paul consumed the combination before he replied.

'I have him fixed for November,' he said then.

'I don't understand that.'

'Bernadette O'Keeffe has Dempsey down for November.'

'Down? What's it mean, down? I'm not asking you about Dempsey.'

'You said would we get him in for the back bedrooms.'

'I'm not talking about the back bedrooms. You know what I'm talking about.'

'Bernadette O'Keeffe has Dempsey booked for the back bedrooms.' Joseph Paul spoke slowly. 'For the month of November,' he said. 'Commencing on the first Monday. Seemingly, he's chock-a-block till then.'

'I'm talking about Ellie Dillahan.'

'What about Ellie Dillahan?'

'You know what about her.'

'I'd say there's a lot being imagined as regards that.'

'Oh, for God's sake, have sense!'

'Ellie Dillahan's a married woman, why'd she be going with a photographer? Dillahan used bring his turf into the yard. Sure, I know him well. Not in a million years would he permit the like of that.'

'Dillahan knows nothing about it, why would he? His wife's being bothered by a scut you wouldn't give tuppence for, and the state she's in you'd hardly get a word out of her. The cut of him on the bicycle with the hat, he's the talk of the town and you're telling me he doesn't exist.'

An extraordinary thing, Joseph Paul considered, his breakfast getting cold. It might be her mother talking, expressions used he hadn't heard since the time of the trouble. The two red spots had appeared high up on her cheeks and he remembered them from childhood. She'd pick up a handful of slack and throw it at you.

'I mentioned it to Ellie myself,' she was saying. 'No option left to me.'

'What'd you say to the poor girl?'

'What had to be said, no more than that. What harm would it do you to say the same to him? Haven't we had eggs from the Dillahans since they were brought in to us on a horse and cart? Then again, there's the turf.'

'You want me to go up to this man on the street?'

'Isn't it something you could say that that orphan girl is a daughter to us?'

The tedium of the conversation had lightened for Joseph Paul with his reflection that their mother's influence and her insistences hadn't entirely left the house, but he was considerably taken aback by the concept of a girl he doubted he'd ever addressed a word to being his daughter.

'What's the matter with you?' He spoke roughly, not meaning to. It would be a terrible thing – and he often thought it – if the peculiarities his sister had acquired over the years turned out to be a creeping dementia. You'd hear of that unfortunate affliction, people would mention a relative. It could be that the running of the house on her own was too much for her. It could be that her delusions about people getting into the picture house ruins had to do with their father being forgotten there on the night of the disaster. She had been their father's pet, as he had been their mother's. That had never been denied by either of them, and it would have been upsetting for her, the way their father would be when he came into the house every night since the time of her trouble – the bloodshot eyes of him, his collar and tie in his pocket, the way he'd start up a foolish whistling in the hall, stumbling and falling down on the stairs, taking money from his wallet and offering it around as a mark of his remorse. He hadn't touched more than a drop or two before the trouble.

His sister was still standing by the breakfast table and Joseph Paul suggested that she should sit down.

'Will I get you water?'

'What'd I want water for?'

'I thought you might.'

'Ask him who he is. Tell him there's talk. What'll happen to the girl when Dillahan washes his hands of her? Where'll she go? Will she walk the roads like poor Orpen Wren? If a child is born, what'll happen then? Take it easy with him, don't abuse him in case he'd hit you. All I'm saying is, explain to him we take an interest in the girl because of the family association. All I'm saying is, ask him straight out what he thinks he's doing. I always liked Ellie.'

'There isn't a word spoken in the back bar of anything awry going on.'

'Who comes into the back bar would know? Aren't the priests bound by the confessional? What I'm saying to you is a person who interferes with another person's funeral should be spoken to, never mind the interest taken in a picture house where a tragedy occurred, never mind he's after a young Catholic girl from the hills.'

She went on talking, repeating everything she'd said already. The fat on Joseph Paul's plate had begun to congeal, a skin had formed on the yolk of his fried egg. The daily girl came in to clear the table.

'I'll make a few enquiries,' he said.

*

The conversation ended with that but later, on his way to his business premises, Joseph Paul reflected that, ever since the upheaval his sister's foolishness had brought about in the house, he had regularly noticed her gazing out of one or other of the front windows and had known what she was looking for. He had seen her polishing the overnight shoes and had conjectured that each pair took on for her the form of Arthur Tetlow's ornamental black brogues – a fantasy that was perhaps the last fantasy left to her and one that in her mind was somehow endangered by what she imagined was going on.

He unlocked the door of the public house while still dwelling on the matter and believing with even greater conviction that the venom directed against a stranger on a bicycle had its source in his sister's betrayal by a traveller in veterinary requisites. Passing through the long street bar, he confirmed to himself his approval of that conclusion, even for a moment feeling sorry for his sister as once he would have.

*

Miss Connulty's interpretation of the breakfast-time contretemps was different. Occupied with changing sheets, she did not regret her anger or wonder why so persistently she had gone on. Her reflections were practical and to the point: she felt better for what had been said. Had she been aware of the contents of her brother's mind during their exchanges she could have told him that in the circumstances dementia was too convenient a term to throw about: she suffered from nothing of the kind, and it was only to be expected that in the normal course of nature she should have developed an interest in the well-being of the girl who delivered eggs to her. There was no more to anything but that.

She finished in one bedroom and began in the next, pulling off the top sheet and then the bottom one, shaking off the pillowslips. She had known what she was doing in giving herself to Arthur Tetlow, and regretted only that she had remained in a house she should not have remained in. Aloud, and firmly, she stated again that she intended to protect Ellie Dillahan in whatever way should be necessary. She gathered up the slept-in sheets, and knocked out four cigarette butts from the bedside ashtray. She propped the window open and settled the blind the way it should be, a little further down to make more of its lace frill.

*

Later that same morning, after Bernadette had been to the back bar with the letters and the cheques, it occurred to Joseph Paul that there might just possibly be another element in his sister's eccentric conduct. Given what she believed was happening between Ellie Dillahan and the man from Castledrummond, she could have worked herself up into a state of resentful jealousy. Her own day was done; she made do with the polishing of other men's shoes.

Affected as the morning advanced by the possible truth of this outcome, Joseph Paul again felt sorry for the sister who had once been his companion. And as if telepathy, long absent between the two, had once more come into play, Miss Connulty on her way downstairs wondered, too, about jealousy. But before the thought could get going, she dismissed it as ridiculous.

15

Florian's passport arrived one morning. The photograph he'd taken of himself had been pasted in, his signature pasted in too, other details completed. *Florian Kilderry. Place of birth: Co. Tipperary. Colour of eyes: Blue. Residence: Ireland.*

It was signed by Kevin Greacen, and he wondered who that was. It was valid for all countries. It was a valuable document. With a golden harp embossed on its green Rexine cover, with *Éire, Ireland, Irlande* on every page, it declared its importance clearly, requesting that the bearer should be offered access to pass freely and be offered all necessary assistance and protection.

Florian put it on the mantelpiece of his bedroom, where he could see it and wouldn't forget where it was. He wiped the mildew from the smallest of the suitcases he had found. He washed it and put it outside the back door to dry in the sun.

In the afternoon of that same day two charity women came for the clothes. Neither death was recent, Florian told them, not that they brought the subject up, but conversation of some kind seemed called for.

'You're on your own?' the one with glasses asked on the way upstairs.

'You're peaceful here,' the other one said, her face familiar but he couldn't place it.

'Yes, it's peaceful.'

He sensed their thinking it was a shame to see the place run down. He opened the wardrobe that had been shared and considered saying it wasn't as strange as it seemed, their clothes kept for so long. But he doubted that he could explain why it wasn't and said nothing.

'The shoes, the shoe-trees?' the woman with glasses enquired. She was the older of the two, with thin grey hair, tall and very upright, as if she'd taught herself to hold on to her posture because she knew that with an effort she could.

'Coat-hangers too?' the other woman asked.

'Everything, if you wouldn't mind.'

'Of course we wouldn't.'

'You're clearing up?'

'The house is being sold.'

Further prospective purchasers had come, the interest in the sale now so keen that the estate agents were increasingly confident of an early offer. The mass of creditors had already been optimistically reassured, a date arranged for a dealer to inspect the remaining furniture in case there was anything of value. A builder's skip had been lowered on to the gravel in front of the hall door and was already almost half full.

Every little helped, the charity women said, thanking him before they left. They mentioned the charities they had in mind for the clothes and, of course, there would be the local poor as well. Florian nodded his understanding of the disposal, imagining his mother's dresses, his father's suits and shoes worn by other people. He waved when the car drove off and the women waved back.

It was more than a fortnight now since he had said the wrong thing in the square in Rathmoye. His clumsiness still nagged, his crassness, as he thought of it, his foolishness. How careless, too, not to notice a wedding ring that was there for anyone to see. He had been casual, even a nuisance in the end, and his regret brought with it an urge to be forgiven, to say that he was sorry.

He carried tennis racquets and umbrellas to the skip, heaved a paraffin heater to it, and buckets with holes in them, paint tins, fire-irons. Then he spread out on the kitchen table one of his father's old Ordnance Survey maps he'd been intending to burn and found on it the Crilly hills and the townland of Cnocrea. He found Lisquin, its two avenues, the gate-lodge on the Kilaney road.

*

Dillahan washed his hands at the sink, scrubbing out the day's dirt. A split in the flesh beside one of his thumbnails was sore when the soap got in, but he didn't remark on it. Years ago his mother had kept ointment for that, but he couldn't remember what it was called.

He asked Ellie if she'd gone in to Rathmoye. He asked about the hook spring in English's. No hurry, he said, no call to go in specially.

'They've ordered it,' she said.

He nodded. He asked if there was a fox about and she said there was, the same one still.

'The dogs were sniffing round the runs first thing. Nothing got in.'

'You're troubled, Ellie.'

'Ah no, no.'

He mentioned Dr Riordan, but she shook her head.

Dillahan was not by nature an inquisitive man, nor did he usually question what bewildered him, accepting his bewilderment for what it was. But it crossed his mind – the first time it ever had – that Ellie was bored, that there was a loneliness about her days at the farmhouse, that housekeeping and eggs, and keeping the dairy spick and span, and whitewashing the turf sheds were not enough. Yet she had never wanted anything besides.

'It's quiet for you,' he said.

'It's all right. Honestly, it's all right.'

'Any time you'd like I'd drive you over to see the nuns in Templeross. Why wouldn't we do that?'

*

The lavender was uncut, the grass untrodden. Waiting at the Lisquin gate-lodge, Florian read *The Brothers Karamazov*. He read for most of the morning but no one came; and passing through Rathmoye again on his way back to his now almost empty house, he read there too, on the seat by the memorial statue in the Square. He lingered there, then rode about, glancing into the shops. He'd almost given up when he was accosted by Orpen Wren, one hand held up in the middle of a street.

'A burden lifted from old shoulders, sir.'

Florian dismounted in a hurry.

'What is, Mr Wren?'

'You have the records back where they belong, sir. An act of goodness, sir.'

About to remind the old man that he hadn't, in fact, accepted the documents he'd been shown when they met before, Florian said instead:

'The drawer of the little table.'

'I rest easy at night, sir, now that they're in the drawer again. I do, sir. I do.'

So fierce was this insistence, so brightly lit the weary eyes, all weariness gone, that Florian's polite lie might have been a statement prompted by the most profound compassion.

'There isn't a book in the library isn't accounted for in the papers, sir. Two years it took me and I mind the time, and the work half done, when the Bishop of Limerick met with a little creature in the salad. The bishop didn't say a word, sir. He put it on the side of his plate and took no notice, not drawing attention to it, nothing like that at all. I never spoke out at the dinner table, it wasn't my place to contribute to any conversation. The time Mrs Colonel Palfrey came she wasn't herself, the Colonel concerned about her. The Misses Uniake wouldn't be separated at the table. Young Cavendish had to have his meat cut. But I was silent at the table always.'

Not interrupting, Florian nodded his receipt of each item as it was completed.

'The butler was Standleby then, sir, an Englishman of Norfolk. Wanted, they said in the kitchen, by the Norfolk constabulary, but I didn't give credit to that. There was resentment in the kitchen quarters, to do with Mr Standleby's ways. The manner he had they called bumptious, but a butler is privileged as to manner, I said myself when the sculleryman Teague would go on about it. Mr Standleby was replaced in the end and Franklin came from the employ of the Villiers-Stuarts.'

'I see.'

'It was indulgence in drink, on Mr Standleby's part, sir.

Well, you'd have heard. As pleasant a disposition as you'd find, but drink was taken on the pantry side of things.'

'Yes.'

'There's never a house the size of Lisquin without you have an upset. The first governess I knew confided that to me. She came into the long room of the library after Macaulay's *Essays*, and I led her to where they were and she made that confidence.'

'I understand.'

'From up at the top of Hurley Lane, sir, you can see the smoke from the Lisquin grates. It is when the smoke isn't there you'd know the coal wasn't delivered, sir.'

'Yes.'

'The smoke's there again, sir.'

'Yes, of course.'

In that same moment Ellie Dillahan passed near them, crossing the street they were in. A van delivering sides of meat was in the way and Florian didn't see her.

*

But she saw Florian. She watched him listening, then holding his hand out and Orpen Wren humbly accepting the ending of the encounter. She loved Florian Kilderry: silently she said that, and said it again while he rode off, out of the Square on to the Castledrummond road.

16

Nettles thrived within the walls that remained. A clump of brambles spread from a corner, sorrel flourished, dandelions gave colour. A door-frame had mostly rotted away, joists hung crookedly. The Lisquin gate-lodge had never had stairs.

Outside, a sheet of corrugated iron, in places eaten by rust, leant against a water-pump. The high gates that opened on to a clay side-road were chained, a farmer's barrier in place across an avenue that went on, to curve away through pasture where cattle grazed.

Florian came often now, but each time saw the lavender still uncut, the grass trodden only where he had walked on it himself. An offer made for the house had been accepted; people no longer came to look it over. He had time on his hands.

Once he rode on to Cnocrea and went by the farm-house, white and tidy, nobody about. He guessed it was the right one but, fearing again to be a nuisance, he rode on and in a roundabout way returned to the gate-lodge. It didn't seem much to ask that he should be allowed to say he was sorry before he left Ireland for ever, but every day he was less hopeful than he'd been the day before. He found a piece of iron and rooted out, as best he could, the ivy that was choking the lavender. He wondered if she would guess when he had gone that it was he who had done that but, after all, why should she?

Then, when he had waited for longer than usual one morning and had decided not to come again, a sound on the road disturbed the silence. There'd never been a sound before. There'd never been anything or anyone.

*

Men clapped while the woman danced. The woman was laughing, her arms thrown out, her scarlet skirt tossed about in the dance, her fair hair wild: the book was face downward on the stubby grass, its coloured cover brightened by the sun. He was kneeling beside it, close to where the lavender grew. He was wearing the hat he'd been wearing the last time.

'Hullo,' he said.

Ellie pushed her bicycle through the gap where once there'd been a postern gate. He took it from her and laid it down beside his.

'Your lavender's dying, did you know?'

'No, I didn't.'

'I've tried to weed it.'

*

She was wearing a different dress, green, in stripes. A handbag was in the basket attached to the handlebars of her bicycle, its shiny black surface gone in places. There were freckles on the bridge of her nose, a few on her forehead. He hadn't noticed them before.

'I didn't mean to distress you that day,' he said. 'I came here a few times. To say I was sorry in case you were ever here too.'

'I shouldn't have gone off like that.'

'It didn't matter.'

'I shouldn't have, though, without a word.'

As she spoke, Florian realized that Ellie Dillahan loved him, and hesitated. Shelhanagh House was almost sold, his passport on the mantelpiece, a suitcase waiting to be packed: he searched for words to say it might be better to end what had not begun. But words eluded him and it was Isabella – her smile, her voice, and she herself in different places – who crowded his thoughts, not this girl who was saying now that if he liked she would show him where the house the old man talked about had been. Again he hesitated and the silence felt longer than he knew it was.

'If you have time for it,' he said at last.

*

They left their bicycles where they were. Yes, she had time, Ellie said as they walked away from them, time enough. It wasn't like being in Rathmoye, on the streets, among people, being frightened. There was a calmness and, as if she were alone, she belonged in its quiet.

He held the barbed wire apart while she scrambled through it, and helped her again where a tree had fallen across the avenue. When he gave her his hand to take it was the first time they had touched, and still the calm was there.

*

'Did you always live in the hills?' he asked. 'Before where you are now?'

'I came to the farm a servant.' From Cloonhill, she said, an institution.

'Are you an orphan?'

'They called us foundlings. At Cloonhill we all were that. Found somewhere.'

They sat down where there was a gateway in the wire fence that ran along the avenue. They leant their backs against the bars of the gate. The cattle in the fields on either side of the avenue were inquisitive, poking at the wire with their heads before they ambled away. Florian searched for cigarettes but there wasn't one left in the packet he found.

'Was it horrible, the institution? Did you hate it?'

'We were always there. The nuns pretended our birthdays, they gave us our names. They knew no more about us than we did ourselves. No, it wasn't horrible, I didn't hate it.'

A horse-dealer's residence Cloonhill had been, left in a will to the convent in Templeross, to be put to charitable use. Its concrete façade was made uglier by institutional severity, the lower panes of uncurtained windows painted white. The horse-dealer's ballroom was still called that, the foundling girls of one time or another clustered around its wood stove on winter evenings, or sitting in twos at desks that had been a gift when they'd become too worn and grimy elsewhere. Upstairs the mattresses had been passed on too. The dining-room's long deal table had, and clothes and tattered schoolbooks had.

Florian entered that cloistered world, footsteps clattering on bare stairs, the murmur of catechism and prayer before another day could properly begin, forgotten porridge acrid on the air. Demure, obedient, fifteen abandoned girls, as many as the house could take, stood silently in line, their washed hands held out, hair cut short, clothes fitting them as best they could. And each girl knelt when another day was over, beside a metal bed, a strip of patterned linoleum tacked down, a single wash-stand shared. Privacy was a nightdress put on before the last of daytime clothes were taken off.

Apples were picked in the horse-dealer's orchard, blackberries from the fields. Potatoes were cultivated, milk supplied as charity from a farm. No man was employed at Cloonhill, a man's assistance begged only when the generator failed or chimneys had to be swept, when pipes froze in winter or wasps in summer made their nests.

The Reverend Mother's visit was in spring; and next there was the August outing, beads told in the sacred ambience of Holycross. They found the carpentry nun: dead in her shed, her eighty-first year not quite achieved, a picture-frame that had come apart still in a vice. You were punished if you repeated bad words. You were punished if you talked to the delivery men, or whispered 'You Are My Sunshine' or 'Bésame Mucho'. You were punished if you danced in the ballroom. You accepted what there was. You were fortunate.

*

Where the avenue ended moss carpeted an empty flatness on which clover was scrappily nourished. Beyond a wicket gate there was a path that disappeared into trees, another way to the house that had been razed. A second avenue, more wildly overgrown, dwindled away, becoming nothing. They went back then.

'Thank you for showing me,' Florian said before they parted.

He watched her going, puffs of dust forming where the

bicycle wheels disturbed the road's dried-up surface. She didn't look back, as she might have. It wasn't her way; already he knew that. The narrow byroad narrowed further and then she was no longer there.

17

The Lisquin gate-lodge became their place. Behind a loose stone in one of the walls there was a cavity where a note might be left should meeting there not be possible as it had been arranged. They lay in sunshine beside the bicycles that were no longer ordinary, having become the means of their being in one another's company. They walked again on the avenue that went nowhere, never venturing beyond the emptiness it led them to, since going further in that direction would have brought them to where cars and tractors went by and where the bunga- lows that were the outskirts of Rathmoye began. It was on the avenue, near the fallen trees, that they first embraced.

While more time passed they discovered the maze at Mount Olery Gardens and the tearooms there which, being for tourists, weren't frequented by local people. They cycled on unmade-up byroads to Enagh, where the Great Cross of the Field was another tourist attraction. They walked in the woods at Lyre, visited the monks' graves at Ballyhayes, climbed up to the standing stones at Gortalassa. They were never again seen in each other's company in Rathmoye.

Although they expected that Orpen Wren would sooner or later appear at Lisquin, he never did. Nor did anyone else, and the sense of being lost in uninterrupted peace became their clandestine sanctuary. And Ellie's stream of recollection, long undisturbed, found life again.

'There isn't much,' she protested when she was asked about coming to the farmhouse.

'Tell me, though.'

'It was the same for all of us when we were sent some-where.'

The nuns would enquire around and then they made the arrangements. When the day came the girls would be in the hall to say goodbye to the one who was going. A girl would be lucky when there'd be a place for her.

'That was said many a time, and you'd always want to go to the house that was got for you. You'd never not want to go. Great store was set on it when everything was fixed, and you'd be excited. We used guess where would it be, a town was what we wanted. Waterford I wanted myself for the sound of it, but they said a farm.'

The more he asked her about her childhood at Cloonhill the more Ellie loved her interrogator. No matter how strange he still sometimes seemed, she felt as if all her life she had known him. The past he talked about himself became another part of her: the games he had played alone, the untidy rooms of the house he described, the parties given, the pictures painted. Being with him in the woods at Lyre, where the air was cold and the trees imposed a gloomy darkness, or walking among the monks' graves, or being with him anywhere, telling or listening, was for Ellie more than friendship, or living, had ever been before.

'A farm,' he prompted in the tearooms at Mount Olery and she said it was Sister Ambrose who told her it was a widowed man she was to go to.

'She said get the girls down to the hall, half five or six the car would come. So we were in the hall, the rain pelting against the windows and the fanlight, and someone looking out saw the car and then the bell wires rattled before the bell rang, the way that always was. And Sister Clare came hurrying to open the front door and a woman came in, rain dripping off her. "We have her ready for you," Sister Clare said, and said to me to step forward. "Are you the the girl then?" the woman asked me and Sister Clare said speak up. The box that had my belongings in it had to be returned and she told the woman and the woman said she'd drop it off when next she'd be passing. "Lift out the box to the car for Ellie," Sister Clare instructed, for that was always done when a girl was going, and it was Rose and Philomena this night who did it. "Ach, you'll settle in grand," the woman said in the car, the windscreen wipers going. One of the man's sisters she was; another of them was waiting in the farmhouse to get a look at me. He carried the box upstairs and his sisters took it away when they left. I knew about the accident at the farm, Sister Ambrose told me. A girl would have to know a thing like that, she said. She'd have to know in case the man would be affected by it. You couldn't call it fortunate, she said, any man widowed, but wasn't there good in it all the same, the way things were now? I didn't mind it was a farm, I never minded that. You get used to a farm's ways in the end.'

'What was the accident?'

'The trailer was loaded and he couldn't see over the top of the load. The fastener of the tail-board was loose and she tried to drop the pin into place while she was holding the baby in her arms.'

He nearly sold up, Sister Ambrose had said, and maybe he wouldn't mention the accident at all, how it happened or anything about it. So much it distressed him, maybe he wouldn't.

'And did he?'

'That first evening he did.'

He had to, was what he said, not knowing the nuns had told her already. He flashed a torch out of the kitchen window at the place on the concrete, a dark mark on it still. He never walked near it, he said. He showed her where everything in the house belonged – jugs and cups on their hooks, the *Old Moore's Almanac* where the insurance money was kept, the keys on the nail by the stairs, the contents of the dresser drawers. He showed her the upstairs, the front sitting-room, the bedroom that would be hers. He asked her could she cook.

A few years went by, Ellie said, and they were like that, only the two of them in the house. Then he asked her would she marry him. He said think it over. He said take her time.

'I wanted Sister Ambrose at the wedding, and Sister Clare with her. But they couldn't come, due to a Retreat again at Fermoy.'

Florian didn't say what he felt: that all that shouldn't have happened, that she shouldn't have been sent into the employ of a haunted man. But he thought it, and he wondered if it showed, although he tried not to let it.

'It's not a terrible place,' Ellie said, as if she knew what he was thinking. 'It's only something happened there.'

18

The dog days of August came; Rathmoye was quiet. Small incidents occurred, were spoken of, forgotten. When there were races near by the bookies stayed at Number 4 – J. P. Ferris, Gangly, McGregor from Clonmel. The priests of the parish catered for the faithful, heard sins confessed, gave absolution, offered the Host; the Church of Ireland's skimpy congregation doggedly gathered for weekly worship. The tinker girls brought their babies to the streets from their wasteland caravans and tents. No crime of a serious nature had been committed in Rathmoye during the summer so far; none was now. In all, twenty-one infants had been born.

Two technicians from a stained-glass studio in Dublin measured the windows that were to be replaced in the Church of the Most Holy Redeemer, and sketches of an Annunciation were admired in the presbytery and later approved by the bishop. The paving stones on both sides of Magennis Street were scheduled to be replaced by the end of October. Permission was given for a neon sign at the radio and television shop in Irish Street above which Bernadette O'Keeffe lived. It was agreed that next year's Strawberry Fair should be one week earlier.

Miss Connulty was right when she'd stated that Florian Kilderry had been noticed in the town, but wrong to suggest there was gossip. There was only her own, her brother its sole recipient. 'To tell you the truth,' he complained to Bernadette O'Keeffe in the back bar, 'she has me demented with it.' He had at last seen for himself the man his sister objected to and he had allocated to Bernadette O'Keeffe the task of discovering what she could about him. Pleased to do so, she set about this with some vigour, regularly receiving details of further exchanges on the subject in Number 4. 'The way it's put to me,' her employer passed on, 'this fellow shouldn't be at large at all.'

The unexpected sympathy for his sister he had experienced on the morning of their first disagreement about Ellie Dillahan had long since receded, to be lost finally in renewed crossness to do with the back bedrooms. Bernadette had not been privy to this particular play of familial emotions; nothing had changed at Number 4 The Square, her view was, except that a man who was unknown in Rathmoye had appeared on the scene. That being so, it seemed relevant to say now that Orpen Wren had identified the man as a member of the St John family, and she said it.

'Not that it's likely,' she added.

The 7-Up already poured, her employer pushed her glass a little closer to her. He displayed no annoyance or concern over this complication in the matter his sister sought information about, and which her perversity would almost certainly make something of.

'Best we'd keep it from her,' he decided after a moment of thought. 'I was saying to her last evening wouldn't she forget the whole issue. I was saying something new might keep her occupied – maybe leather-craft or a little flower garden out the back.'

'A flower garden would be nice for Miss Connulty all right.'

'I could be talking to the cat.'

Miss O'Keeffe nodded. She would have given a lot for a nip of John Jameson in the bitter-sweet cordial, but did not say so. She spread out the unsigned cheques and pushed them across the table. He had been lonely since his mother was taken; every day you could see it. In the evenings he went for a walk out on the Nenagh road and ended up in the cemetery again. Weekends, it was the same.

'I only mentioned the St Johns thing in case it fitted in.'

'You were right enough to say it, Miss O'Keeffe. Did McCaffreys' cheque come?'

'Well, no, not yet.'

'We'll give them another day or two. Would you say we would?'

He always asked for her view. These days he was treated less than an overnight man, she'd heard it said, the maid casual with him. She often wondered did he sleep well.

She gathered her papers together, counting the cheques as she slipped them into a fastener. She would let it go until Thursday, she agreed; then she'd send McCaffreys a reminder.

*

In time Bernadette's enquiries bore fruit and through them Miss Connulty learnt that the man she'd taken against went about on a bicycle because it was thought he couldn't drive a car, that he had no visible means of support, was currently engaged in the selling of a house he had inherited, and was planning to emigrate. His identity was established, his name passed on to her, his connection with the St John family dismissed. In Castledrummond he was said to keep himself to himself.

'Not in Rathmoye he doesn't,' Miss Connulty retorted with razor sharpness. 'Not by a long chalk.'

'I'm only telling you what's reported.'

The conversation took place in the big front room, Joseph Paul in an armchair with the newspaper he'd been reading open on his knees, his sister standing by the mantelpiece.

'Have you had words with him?' she asked.

'I have no intention of approaching this man in any way whatsoever. There isn't a reason in the wide world why I should cause offence to a man I don't know just because he rides his bicycle through the town.'

'He's trying something on with Ellie Dillahan. You can tell it by the way of her.'

'There's no reference in what Miss O'Keeffe found out that this fellow is after any woman.'

'Whatever state that girl's in, she's not in it for nothing.'

'We don't know anything about what state Ellie Dillahan is in. You're confused about the entire matter. This fellow's a separate entity altogether from Ellie Dillahan.'

'Have you no pity in you at all? Have you no pity for Dillahan, what he's been through? She found a home with him, the two of them suited in misfortune, and the next thing is you have an interloper up to no good.'

Miss Connulty didn't listen when her brother again refuted that, gesturing with his hands, explaining something she didn't want to hear. You couldn't blame him, he understood nothing. Since the day he'd been born he'd been protected and cosseted, the world withheld from him. Word would get to Dillahan about his young wife's infatuation and who'd blame him for what would happen next?

'If Dillahan turns her out she'll come here,' Miss Connulty promised with sudden, fierce determination. 'Ellie Dillahan will live in this house and hold her head up.'

19

One of the yard doors had worked itself loose from the higher of its two hinges and Dillahan raised it, settling it on a couple of logs and steadying it with a prop.

The screws came out easily. He marked with the point of a bradawl a new position for the hinge and pierced the wood of the jamb just deep enough to hold the screws in place before he drove them in.

'Come November, we'll renew the creosote. Did we do it last year? I doubt we did.' He swung the door. 'How's that then?'

But Ellie, who had been in the yard, had gone back to the house. Standing a little to one side of the kitchen window, she watched her husband returning the logs he had used to the woodshed, then gathering up his tools. She willed him to hurry, to get on with it, to go. Impatience kept her at the window, concealed from the yard because of the way she stood, close to the wall. It wouldn't take a minute, he had said, but he'd been there an hour, his sandwiches made and in the tractor, his flask filled. He would be all day in the fields, he'd said earlier, the brambles to clear, and rotavating the arable.

He came into the kitchen although there was no need to. 'It's all there in the tractor,' Ellie said, thinking when she heard herself that he wouldn't ever have heard her speaking so curtly before, but he appeared not to notice.

He delayed for another ten minutes, looking for something in one of the dresser drawers and not finding it. He said what he had said already about the brambles and the arable.

From the window she watched while he dragged the rotavator out of its shed and coupled it behind the tractor. When he'd driven off, taking the dogs with him, her impatience still lingered. It was alien to her and she hated it.

*

Florian had not revealed that Shelhanagh had been up for sale and now was sold; or that as soon as it was no longer his he would leave Ireland. Time after time, walking among the monks' graves or on the Lisquin avenue, or in the tearooms or at Enagh, he had resolved that before they parted he would say at last what must be said. But time after time he hadn't. Was it reluctance to cause pain that influenced his silence? Or a reluctance to bring abruptly to an end a liaison that had differently begun and now was pleasure? Or was it simply that his fondness for concealment had taken charge, as often in the past it had? He didn't know. When he procrastinated it felt right to do so, yet he knew that what he withheld did not belong to him and would happen anyway, brushing him aside.

Waiting this morning on the lower slopes of Gortalassa, by the red barn where they had agreed to meet, he became more urgently aware of that, and Ellie's lateness brought time's dominance to mind: there was less of it left than he'd imagined.

Still waiting, he saw her in the distance. How well he knew her now, he reflected. Her grey-blue eyes, the softness of her lips, her voice, her smile, her shy composure.

Which dress would it be today? he had become used to wondering before they met, and did so again. The blue, the green, the one with the honeysuckle pattern? How well he knew the bangle that had been her husband's wedding present, the Woolworth's brooch the nuns had given her, her battered handbag. How well he knew the innocence and the gentleness that first had stirred his sympathy and still did.

They pushed their bicycles on the track that began beside the barn. Today they would climb higher than they had when they'd been to Gortalassa before: they hoped to reach the corrie lakes.

They left their bicycles where the track petered out and climbed up to the ring of standing stones. While they rested there, he told her.

'But why?' she asked. 'Why are you going away?'

'When the house is sold there'll be nowhere for me to live in Ireland.'

'I didn't know your house was for sale.'

'There are debts that have to be paid.' He paused a moment. 'It would have spoilt our summer if I had told you earlier.'

She looked away and he knew she was afraid to ask how long they had left.

'The rest of summer,' he said as if she had. 'There'll be a date. Oh, ages off. October perhaps.'

'Is that when you'll be going?'

'Yes, it is.'

He watched a jet plane trailing its ribbon of white against the washed-out paleness of the sky. He watched the white evaporating, the last of its shreds falling apart.

'Is it for ever you'll be going?'

'It is for ever.'

'Like the St Johns?'

'Yes, I suppose so.'

Larks flitted from one high stone to another. Above a carcass not yet picked over a buzzard was stationary in the air. Higher on the hillside a lone sheep moved slowly.

'Don't be unhappy, Ellie.'

She shook her head. She didn't speak.

'I had to tell you.'

'I know you did. I know.'

They climbed through ferns and bracken, the bog-land dry. They skirted an escarpment because it was a shorter way. A distant Angelus bell chimed faintly in the stillness.

*

He would go and that he was gone would be her first thought every morning, as her first thought now was that he was here. She would open her eyes and see the pink-washed walls as she saw them now, the sacred picture above the empty grate, her clothes on the chair in the window. He would be gone, as the dead are gone, and that would be there all day, in the kitchen and in the yard, when she brought in anthracite for the Rayburn, when she scalded the churns, while she fed the hens and stacked the turf. It would be there in the fields, and with her when she stood with her eggs waiting for the presbytery hall door to open, and while Miss Connulty counted out her coins and the man with the deaf-aid looked for insulation guards or udder pads. It would be there while she lay down beside the husband she had married, and while she made his food and cut his bread, and while the old-time music played.

'Do you want to go?' she asked.

'Everything is over for me in Ireland now.'

'I wish you weren't going.'

*

They reached the corrie lakes. The summer they had known and still knew now would never not be theirs, Florian said – the dusky woods at Lyre, the maze at Olery, the lavender, the butterflies. His Cloonhill, what he had made of it, her Shelhanagh. 'All that,' he said. Memory did not let go.

He knew it wasn't solace, but he could do no better. Despair could not be blown away and, although he didn't want to, he remembered his when he blurted out what for so long he had concealed. They had been reading in the garden and they went on reading afterwards, and Isabella said nothing.

Above the three small lakes, hardly more than pools, the bleak rockface was sheer. Out of the sun's reach, the water was dark and icy still. There were no birds, no other life, no sound. It was a place he might have come to when he fumbled with photography, Florian thought. But memory would more tellingly preserve it.

Their faces were cold against each other for a moment before they parted. Where would he go? she asked.

'Perhaps Scandinavia,' he said.

*

On the way back to Shelhanagh, Florian called in at the Dano Mahoney public house. Two drinkers at the bar looked up, interrupting a conversation about greyhounds. The ex-pugilist landlord nodded a curt welcome. Florian took his glass to the corner table he had occupied on the day of Mrs Connulty's funeral.

137

His father had first brought him here, the landlord different then, a friendlier man whom his father had seemed to know well. A few days after his mother's death that was, a time when his father kept saying he needed a drink. There had been reminiscences then too, of Italy, of love, of finding the house when they ran away to Ireland, of the legacy that came eventually from Genoa and how that had felt like being paid to stay away so as not to be an embarrassment to the Verdecchias. 'I always liked the Verdecchias, though,' his father confessed. 'Because they were her people, I think.'

Born a Catholic but lapsing in her faith, Florian's mother had been buried in the small Protestant churchyard in Castledrummond so that when the time came she and his father would not be separated. 'We liked arranging things,' his father said in the Dano Mahoney Bar. 'We enjoyed all that.' Isabella hadn't come to either funeral. Florian had thought she would.

Of the two, he was the less good painter, his father used to say, but Florian now could not separate the watercolours that were left behind into who had painted which. Nor could he, sometimes, separate his mother and father as people, for with the years they had grown alike, although they had themselves insisted that once they'd been quite notably different and given to disagreement.

'He's asking near four hundred for his animal.' The voice of one of the drinkers carried from the bar and then was hushed. Another man came in. He asked to use the telephone because a bullock had fallen down a ravine.

Florian finished his wine and his cigarette and then he cycled on. He would have to see to the grave before he left, and he wondered who would do that when he did go.

He was hungry and went round by the Greenane half-and-half for bread and porksteak, and to arrange with Mrs Carley to leave the hall-door key with her when the day came. Riding on to Shelhanagh afterwards, he realized that his nostalgic reflections in the roadside bar had been an effort to brush away an uneasy day. It was no more than the truth that he had sought to prolong a friendship which summer had almost made an idyll of. But what he had failed to anticipate was the depth of disappointment its inevitable end would bring. He had allowed the simple to be complicated. He had loved being loved, and knew too late that tenderness in return was not enough. 'Dear Flor, what a muddle you are!' Isabella's favourite word for him, repeated often in Italian and in English with cousinly affection. He had liked the word then; he didn't now.

*

That night, in her sleep, Ellie wept. She tried to wake up in case her sobs were heard. She could hear them herself but when she managed to rouse herself she found her husband undisturbed. Her pillow was wet and she turned it over, and in the morning her tears had gone as if she had imagined them, but she knew she hadn't.

20

A few days after his revelation that he was to leave Ireland Florian found, beneath a pile of straw fish baskets in what had once been a pantry, a leatherbound record book he had years ago concealed there. He gathered up the mildewed baskets to take to his garden bonfire and saw again the handsomely embossed lettering: *The Huntsman's Fieldbook*. He had hidden it and couldn't remember where, had repeatedly searched the house before giving up.

He turned pages that were familiar to him, at the bottom of each a tidily boxed paragraph of printed notes, with occasionally an illustration, concerning the nature and habitat of various forms of wildlife, its preservation or destruction. The only handwriting, on faint grey lines, was his own.

He threw the fish baskets on to his fire and, watching the straw blaze up, remembered being ashamed to tell Isabella when she returned to Shelhanagh the following summer that he'd forgotten where he'd hidden the *Fieldbook*, saying instead that he had thrown it away. Isabella hadn't been entirely blameless in all this herself. There always was a rush at the end of her July visits. This time, her luggage in the hall, she had left the *Fieldbook* on her bed and, discovering later that she had, fiercely instructed Florian to see to its concealment. It was important, or seemed so then, since secrecy came into so much of what she and Florian did.

In the kitchen he shook the dust from the pages and wiped the leather cover with a damp cloth. His handwriting hadn't changed with the passage of time. Square and firm, in clear black ink, it still was that. Seven years ago it was, Florian calculated, and was just beginning to read how he had filled the blankness above some information about the feeding practices of the carp when the hall-door bell sounded, accompanied by a brisk knocking.

'Well, here we are!' A tall man smiled and bowed when Florian opened the door. A woman, brightly dressed, was there also.

'Here indeed!' she exclaimed. 'And poor Mr Kilderry doesn't know us from Adam!'

They didn't give a name but Florian remembered seeing their black shooting-brake drawn up a few weeks ago.

'I think you came to see the house,' he said.

'Oh, better than that,' the tall man corrected him. 'We bought it.'

He extended a hand. The woman, whom Florian assumed to be his wife, pressed a wine merchant's carrier bag on him, saying it contained something refreshing.

'We wondered if we might snoop about a bit,' she murmured in a tinkling voice.

'Of course. I'm sorry I couldn't place you. A lot of people came.' Champagne he guessed their gift was. He thanked them, although he didn't like champagne.

'What a happy day!' the woman exclaimed. She smiled

at Florian, her manner playful. 'Do please forgive us for being a bore!'

'Those gorgeous scenes!' the man contributed, referring to the unframed watercolours in the drawing-room while he unfolded a typewritten sheet. 'Unforgettable!'

'What a *very* happy day!' his wife continued to enthuse, and Florian wondered if she was drunk.

He left them to look about as they wished and to take measurements. He didn't return to the *Fieldbook* he'd found but went on throwing anything that would burn on to his fire and anything that wouldn't into the skip. He came across his father's binoculars, which had been lost also, and an umbrella someone had left behind and never come back for. He found the key that wound the clock in the hall but hadn't done so for years. He found the beads of a necklace in a matchbox.

The afternoon he'd hidden the *Fieldbook* under the fish baskets he had come down the back stairs with it in his hand, not taking it to his bedroom because there wasn't time, since Isabella would miss her train if everyone didn't hurry. The door of the poky room that was then a pantry was open. All that came clearly back again, as if it had never not been there.

He had appropriated the *Fieldbook* in the first place when it fell out of a stack of *National Geographic* magazines in the garage. He hadn't been interested in the wildlife details but the faintly lined pages attracted him as much as the leather cover did and in time he found a use for them. Isabella, who often poked about among his possessions, was surprised by what she found written there. '*Bizzarro!*' her comment was.

The women passed by Miss Dunlop on their way to the kitchen, both of them smirking a little. The Wing Commander moved close to Miss Dunlop and whispered in her ear some words of love. Miss Dunlop blushed, for the Wing Commander had put his earthy desires regarding Mrs Meade into words. He imagined it was Mrs Meade's ear he spoke into, and he imagined biting the lobe of the countrywoman's ear and feeling her coarse hair on his cheek.

'It's all very well,' Miss Dunlop protested, sensing at last that something was amiss. She found a cigarette in the pocket of her suit and lit it.

'How much you are the world to me!' the Wing Commander murmured, reaching for her again.

No one else except Isabella had ever known about the writing in the *Fieldbook*, or even that the *Fieldbook* still existed. Nor did Florian himself regard his fragments of composition as anything more than the fruits of idleness. Nothing was complete, bits of people, bits of occurrences, and he noticed now that the writing was in places uncertain, his adolescent creations often verging on the affected. Madame Rochas, an old schoolteacher, was 'haunted by footsteps ceaseless in the night'. Yu Zhang was so delighted by *Circus of Horrors* that he could not pass a cinema where it was showing without seeing it yet again. The Sunday visitors of Anna Andreyev spoke of St Petersburg and Lermontov. Emmanuel Quin was no more than a name, as Johnny Adelaide was, and Vidler. The Reverend Unmack stole from counters and did not know himself.

'Mr Kilderry!'

Florian went upstairs.

'Your hot press,' the tall man said.

'The hot press?'

'It seems a trifle damp.'

'Well, yes, it is.'

'A leak? We wondered.'

'I'm afraid so. I'm sorry about it.'

'My dear fellow!'

Florian smiled and nodded, and went away. 'What'd he have to say for himself?' he heard the woman ask when he was on his way downstairs. 'Couldn't care less,' the man reported.

They stayed all afternoon, but did not again enquire about the defects they came across. Eventually they called out to say they'd finished and were effusive in their gratitude as they said goodbye. Then they drove off in their big black shooting-brake and Florian returned to the pages of the *Fieldbook*. Most of what he read he had forgotten writing.

On Madole's wasteland Willie John and Nason didn't notice the boy at first. Then Willie John did.

'What's the kid want?' he asked.

'Only to watch,' Nason said.

The Sky Wasp spluttered and glided back to them, the engine dead because the lighter fuel had run out.

'We could charge the kid for watching.' Willie John laughed, his big jaw split, the freckles around his eyes merging as the flesh puckered. He was red-haired and ungainly. Nason was thin and small, with a lick of black hair trailing over his forehead, his clothes always tidy. He was the younger by a few months.

'I'll tell you what it is,' Nason said. 'The kid's over at the gravel

pits. He's run off from the travelling people. There's underground places at the pits. That kid's grubbing for food with the rabbits.'

Florian hadn't liked Isabella reading his jottings. But she had, and wanted to know who the people were and where they had come from, why sentences and words often broke off unfinished when sometimes half a page was filled.

At Euston station Michael decided that this was best: to ask straight out and be told, anything rather than the absurdity of making a journey that was unnecessary.

'Clione?' he said when the ringing tone ceased and his sister's voice came on.

'You'll come, Michael? All the time he asks.'

But what on earth good would it do? Either way, what good? The long overnight haul and arriving in the early morning at the dreary railway station with his pyjamas and razor in a carrier bag because he didn't possess a suitcase. And turning into the driveway. He hated turning into the driveway most of all.

'He's dying now,' his sister said.

But at Euston station people were waiting to use the phone. Michael put the receiver down.

Isabella insisted that Florian abandoned too much too easily, often flippantly. In their disagreement about that, she was cool and unflurried, Florian impatient and at a disadvantage because he was flattered that she minded so much. She quoted back to him with admiration what he had written. About cities he had never been to, misfortunes he hadn't experienced. About rejection and despair.

About Olivia, searching London for a man she loved, who stole from her.

He might have gone to Spain. He'd gone to Spain before without a word. Someone he knew had a house in Spain, or rented a house there, she wasn't sure which. On the other hand, now and again he left London in order to stay with people in different parts of the country. 'Hasn't been in,' the barman in the George said. Olivia asked other drinkers there and they said they hadn't seen him. She reassured them because of course it would be all right. It would be Spain and he'd be back. He wasn't in the Coach and Four. He wasn't in the Queen and Knave.

A girl suggested the Zinzara Club and they went there with a lanky woman the girl knew, and a man with a bow tie. Derek was on the door tonight, his hair done in a different way, and when Olivia asked the woman behind the bar she shook her head and Olivia went to the Grape and he was there, standing where he'd been standing the night she first saw him. He was with people she didn't know, as he'd been then. She saw him seeing her, but he didn't move and then the people he was with stared at her and no one spoke.

Surely, Isabella urged, he could make something of that, since he had made a little of it already? 'Oh, please, why not?' she begged, determinedly, repeatedly. 'Oh, please.'

He knew he couldn't.

*

While Jessie scurried among the reeds Florian smoked and watched the night beginning. He wished Isabella could know the huntsman's book hadn't been thrown away and now was resurrected. He wished she could be here as so often she had been, by the lake, the dark creeping on, more secrecy pretended than was necessary. He wondered if she had married Signor Canepaci or someone else; he wondered if she was happy. He had exasperated her, not being able to tell her who Olivia was, or who Miss Dunlop was, or any of the others. 'Did they come to the parties?' she asked. Were Nason and Willie John boys at school? Was Madole's wasteland somewhere they could go?

Florian did not try to sleep that night. He didn't go to bed and in his silent house what he had been separated from for so long seemed tonight more than he had written down. Miss Dunlop's blouse was pink, a touch of henna transformed her hair. The pale, stretched features of Yu Zhang lost their solemnity in a smile. The Wing Commander had experienced gaol. An injury, not yet healed, was vivid on the forehead of the boy at the gravel pits. The old teacher's nightly footsteps were the footsteps of a child whose fate she dared not think about. Life wasn't worth living, Olivia whispered.

Reading and rereading the scraps he had given up on, Florian did not readily conclude that time, in passing, had brought perception, only that his curiosity was stirred by the shadows and half-shadows imagination had once given him, by the unspoken, and what was still unknown. He added nothing to what was written, only murmuring occasionally a line or word that might supply an emphasis or clarify a passage.

But in the early morning, standing at the water's edge while in vain he scanned the sky for the bird that no longer came, he felt exhilarated, as if something had happened to him that he didn't entirely know about, or know about at all. This feeling was still there when he returned to the house, while he made coffee and toasted bread, and gave his dog her food. It was there when, later in the morning, he lay down to sleep. He slept all day, and woke to it.

21

Ellie had not been to the gate-lodge since before the day they had climbed up to the corrie lakes at Gortalassa. It was a busy time of year, made more so by helping at the Corrigans' harvest: it wasn't as easy as it had been to get away.

Her low spirits at Gortalassa had not revived, although they did a little when, behind the loose stone in the wall at the ruins, she found a note that gave directions of how to get to Shelhanagh House. *Come any day you can. Come any time*, the message was, on the back of a map, in handwriting she had not known before. The ease with which all this happened – the note written, the directions given, the map drawn, his wanting her to come to the house he talked so much about – gave Ellie more than hope, restoring something at least of what had been taken from her on the slopes of Gortalassa. It had not before been suggested that she should make the journey he suggested now, and she wondered if it could be that for some reason everything was suddenly different. That the sale of the house had fallen through. That the people buying it had made a mistake or, when they calculated, didn't have the money. Months, maybe a year, might pass while the unsold house kept him in Ireland. She had thought she might never hear from him again. But she had and he wanted her to come to him.

Thursday I'll come. The afternoon is better.
She left her note where his had been.

*

To arrange the loan with which he hoped to buy Gahagan's field Dillahan made one of his rare weekday visits to Rathmoye. In Mr Hassett's small private office he presented the facts and Mr Hassett said he didn't think two thousand pounds was going to break the bank. Beneath his small moustache he fleetingly displayed the smile familiar to borrowers when he agreed to make a loan. Dillahan nodded his gratitude.

'A pity to pass it by,' he said.

'It's always a pity to pass good land by, Mr Dillahan.'

'The trouble is, one day he'd be on about offers for it, the next he'd be talking about clearing and draining.'

'He's neglected it, has he?'

'Well, yes.'

'The older a man is the harder it is for him to part with what he has. And the more reason he should. Not that selling out isn't hard on any man, never mind his years.'

'Gahagan has a fair bit left, all the same.'

Dillahan stood up. There was a golf cup on the desk and Mr Hassett saw him looking at it. A bit of luck, he said, the Rathmoye Bankers' Prize. He held the door of his small private office open. The two men shook hands and Dillahan passed through the main offices, out into the sunshine of the Square. He looked to see if Ellie had come back from her shopping. One of the back doors of the Vauxhall was open, a basket and two bags still on the ground beside where she stood. The mad old Protestant was talking to her.

*

'They went because of it,' Orpen Wren said. 'The St Johns didn't have control over their sons.'

Ellie nodded. She read her list again, making sure she'd got everything.

'The last steward they had at Lisquin was Mr Boyle and the mistress had himself and myself brought to her little room. "Close the door," she said, and I did and Mr Boyle didn't say a word. Men coming to the house looking for their women, she said. Wives or daughters, it never mattered. The Rakes of Mallow weren't in it, she said. "Oh, worse," she said. "Worse than that any day."

'The master had taken to his bed for the shame of it, and she came out with it then: that Elador was gone off with a woman. "All I know is the running of the house," she said. "I can't be devising stratagems." Her two little girls were a few years old and Jack maybe fourteen. What good was she for more besides that, was what she was asking us, and Mr Boyle said he'd scour all Ireland. He'd take a stableman with him and they'd go into every inn and hotel. They'd search the two of them out if it took them a six-month. He wouldn't spare Elador, he promised her that. He'd have it clear and plain with Elador that he must give the woman back where she belonged. Mr Boyle said to the mistress, "Ma'am, I'd maybe have to thrash it out of Elador." He said he'd need her permission for laying hands on her boy, and the master's permission, because he'd be frightened of the law. She said it again that her husband was in his bed. She was beside herself, she didn't remember telling us before. "Mr Wren will write it down," Mr Boyle said. "Mr Wren will write it down that Elador came back chastened to Lisquin. Mr

Wren will put the date to it. And write it down that permission was given."'

Ellie tried to detect from her husband's gait if he'd been
allowed the loan, but she couldn't tell. A shawled woman
held out a hand and when he'd reached into his pockets he
dropped a coin into it.

'Her heart was broken for Lisquin, Mr Boyle said. Her
heart was broken for the St Johns brought low by a son.
"It's in this family always," she said, and there were tears
on her face. For a long time already it was in the family,
she said, one generation to the next. "Let me go, ma'am,"
Mr Boyle begged her. "Let the stableman and myself make
an end of the unworthiness of the whole thing." If afterwards the story would be told, Mr Boyle said, if afterwards
the children of the St Johns would hear before they became
men of how Elador St John had been thrashed in Letter-
kenny or Arklow or by the roadside in County Clare, how
he and his woman were hunted down like two wild crea-
tures by dogs – if the children would be told the story, that
would be an end to it for ever. And when himself and the
stableman went they found the two in Portumna by the
river, in lodgings where spalpeens would stay, or labour-
ing men on the repair of a road. They gave the woman
back to her husband, and Elador St John was sent out of
Ireland. But one night, when years again had passed, a
farmer came to Lisquin with a gun, which was taken off
him or he'd have shot Jack dead. The day following there
was no one in the household that didn't know the St Johns
would go.'

His eyes had become steely and intense. One hand
gripped the top of the car's open door. All during his long

monologue Ellie had had the impression that he was trying to say something else and couldn't manage to because he couldn't find the words. He asked her if she understood.

'Lisquin's gone this long time, Mr Wren,' she said. 'The St Johns with it.'

'"We know old trouble, sir," I said to George Anthony the first day he was back with us. It was the trouble brought the family down, lady, only that wouldn't be said unless it was within the walls of Lisquin. That's how it is to this time, lady.'

'Yes.'

'The papers are back where they belong. He was good to take them from me. An old ghost, they'd say, if they saw me coming with them myself. I wouldn't presume to be welcome in the house. George Anthony saw me right.'

'Who you're talking about isn't a St John, Mr Wren.'

'There's your husband coming now, lady. I know your husband well.'

*

Dillahan waited for a car to pass before he began to cross the Square and then was delayed by Fennerty the cattle auctioneer, who told him Con Hannington was dead. 'Last evening,' he said.

'I heard.'

They talked for a few minutes. Poor Con had been shook a long time, Fennerty said, and Dillahan kept nodding, trying to edge away. He didn't like coming in to Rathmoye because he still sensed the pity of people, and since he continued to blame himself for the accident it came naturally to him to assume that in spite of their sympathy others blamed him too. On Sundays he went to early Mass because it was less crowded.

He said he'd see Fennerty around. When he reached the Vauxhall Ellie was alone again.

'That's fixed,' he said. 'Have you everything?'

'I have.'

'We'll be off so.'

He eased the Vauxhall through the other cars in the Square and drove across Magennis Street into Cashel Street.

'What'd the old fellow want?'

'Only rambling on,' Ellie said, 'you wouldn't know what he was at.'

'It can't be much of a joke, your memory turned inside out for you.' He stopped for a woman and a pram at a crossing. 'Poor old devil.'

'Yes.'

They passed the two churches, then left the town behind. They waited at temporary traffic lights where the road was up.

'Who's that?' Dillahan asked when they passed a cyclist.

She wanted to say it was Florian Kilderry and that she was in love with him. She wanted to say the name, to say he was on the road because he was going to the back gate-lodge of Lisquin House, where often they were together. She wanted to say he would find a note from her, that he would have come for that.

'I don't know who he is,' she heard herself saying, and again there was the urge to talk about him. She'd seen him about before, she said. Florian Kilderry she'd heard him called. Near Castledrummond he came from.

The lights changed. They waited for a lorry coming slowly. Dillahan said there used to be a County Council foreman called Kilderry, two fingers gone from his right hand. He said his father once bought a scarifier at a bankrupt sale in Castledrummond.

'I remember coming back from school and it was in the yard.' He had never been in Castledrummond himself.

'No.'

'It was busy today, was it?'

'It was, for a Tuesday.'

'I see there's posters up, some old circus coming.'

'They've been up a while.'

'Not Duffy's, though?'

'No, not Duffy's.'

'I used be taken to Duffy's.'

He had told her about that when first she came to the farm, how he'd always been impatient, waiting for the elephants to come on, and how a clown had persuaded one of his sisters to give him a kiss. He had told her about Piper's Entertainments when they'd come to Rathmoye, the roundabouts and bumper cars, the hoopla stall where he'd won a china rabbit.

'Con Hannington's funeral's Friday,' he said. He drew out to turn to the right, and waited for a tractor to go by. He saluted the man on it.

'Con lent me fifty pounds one time,' he said. 'The barley failed and I was pushed.'

He would have paid the money back, every penny, and Con Hannington would have known he would. The bank wasn't taking a chance with the loan and the bank would know that too.

'I'll go to the funeral,' he said.

She hadn't often left a note, always managing to come herself, always wanting to. He'd be there by now and he'd maybe wait a while, then he'd lift out the stone. He hadn't realized whose car it was when it went by. He didn't know the car.

They passed Gahagan's gate, beside the old milk-churn platform that was falling to bits, then the turn-off to the boreen that was the way up to the hills, difficult in winter when a flood came down it.

They had to back for the post van, and the new young postman wound his window down and handed out the bill for the fertilizer that had been delivered a few weeks ago.

'A decent lad, that,' her husband said.

The dogs heard the car's approach and began to bark when it was still far off. As well she'd looked behind the stone; as well he'd come to look there today. A Golden Eagle his bicycle was called, a picture of an eagle on a rock below the handlebars. She'd never known a bicycle called that before.

'There's the last of the potatoes to lift,' her husband said, 'before we'd get the rain. Only a dozen or so rows.'

'I'll help you so.'

'Arrah, no, you have enough to do.'

'I never mind.'

'Ah, well, no.' He protested softly, shaking his head as he often did when she offered to do what he considered she no longer should.

He turned the car into the yard. The dogs came to greet them.

22

Shelhanagh House was not as Ellie had imagined it. A white hall door was tinged with watery green, the paint worn away in places. On the gravel an iron container was beginning to overflow, heaped with tattered suitcases gnawed by mice, rusty paint tins, an ironing-board, weighing-scales, a typewriter, electric fires, a fender, a press for trousers. The flagstones in the hall weren't covered, the dining-room contained no furniture, the drawing-room was not a drawing-room.

'I should have warned you,' he said.

He led the way upstairs, past empty rooms, to what he called the high attics, to a narrow stairway that then became a ladder to the lofts and the roof. They stood on the warm lead of a gully between two slated inclines, looking down at the garden and, beyond it, to the lake Ellie had been told about, over farmland to the distant mountains. A tractor moved slowly up and down a field, soundless where they stood.

'I always liked it up here,' he said and he pointed places out and gave them names – Greenane Crossroads, a bridge a little further off, on the way to Castledrummond, and farms and houses. 'I used to read here. For hours, you know, in summer.'

'It's lovely. Everywhere.'

A dog followed them when they were downstairs again.

'Jessie she's called,' he said, and in the kitchen picked up a book from the table. A long time ago he'd lost it and found it only the other day. He hated losing things, he said.

'Is the house still being sold?' Ellie asked, reaching down to stroke the dog's head when they were in a cobbled yard.

'Poor old Jessie's getting on a bit,' he said. 'Yes, Shelhanagh is sold.'

If the sale fell through she had promised herself to make her confession. She had promised atonement, and obedience; that she would, for all her life, in every hour of every day, be ordered by obedience.

'The seventeenth of next month,' he said.

Ages, he'd said before, since there were so many formalities. October perhaps, and she had imagined the bare trees of autumn, the mists of November gathering while he still was here. September the seventeenth was less than three weeks away.

'The same afternoon I found that book the people who've bought Shelhanagh came. An excitable pair,' he said.

'I thought maybe something might go wrong.'

'No, nothing did.'

In the yard the rickety doors of a garage had to be lifted up when they were being pulled open. It was a long time since this car had been on a road, he said. He called the motor car a Morris Cowley and opened at the back what he called a dicky seat.

In the garden he pointed at long grass shimmering in the sunlight, swaying a little because a breeze had got up.

'That's where the tennis court was.'

He'd had a tutor for a while, he said, who played tennis in his ordinary shoes. His father considered that wasn't the thing at all. Even with his limp, his father had always won at tennis.

Every summer the man who used to shoot the rabbits took away the dead ones, but others came. In the rhodo-dendron shrubbery there was a secret place and a rabbit would sometimes run out of it as if, for rabbits, it was a secret place too.

'I had imaginary friends there and once pretended that the rabbit man shot one of them by mistake. I had a funeral, with wreaths of rhododendron.'

Wisps of smoke blew about. In cardboard boxes beside a heap of smouldering ashes separate bundles of papers were held together by rubber bands, and there were cheque-book stubs and letters in their envelopes, and receipts on spikes. Ellie watched a blaze beginning and remembered the letter she'd written to Sister Ambrose, which she had burnt in the Rayburn. Longer ago than three weeks that was, months more like. Three weeks was nothing.

He threw more paper on to the fire, and then the boxes themselves. He pointed at the roof of the house, a differ-ent part of it from where they had stood: people who'd come to a party had climbed up there and one of them sang a song there, a man who sang in operas.

'Is it definite?' she asked. 'September the seventeenth?'

'Yes, it's definite.'

Wild sweet pea was in bloom, white and faded shades of mauve and pink. Apples were forming on the trees they passed among on their way to the lake. At its edge, water rats scuttled into the water when the dog came snuffling through the reeds.

'A Thursday,' she said. 'The seventeenth of September.'

*

There was a dullness in her voice. He heard it and wished she was not here, although he wanted her to be. Being here made everything worse for her: he could tell, and knew she couldn't because she didn't want to. He hadn't known himself when he'd suggested that she should come.

'There wasn't any other way,' he said. 'It had to be sold. I didn't realize things would go so smoothly.'

Almost everything sounded wrong as soon as he said it and for a moment he felt that he belonged in his own created world of predators, that he was himself a variation of their cruelty. He had taken what there was to take, had exorcized, again, his nagging ghost. And doing so, in spite of tenderness, in spite of affection for a girl he hardly knew, he had made a hell for her.

*

She watched him rooting for a cigarette and finding one loose in a pocket. She watched him straightening it, packing the shreds of tobacco in. Then they went back the way they had come, through the apple trees. In the garden he threw a ball for his dog. In the kitchen he showed her a faded postcard that had been propped up on a windowsill. A woman in old-fashioned clothes had a quill in one hand and what might have been a saucer in the other. A monk was praying.

'St Lucy,' he said.

The handle of a dagger and part of its blade protruded

160

from the saint's neck. There was no blood. She had a halo.

'You have a look of this St Lucy,' he said.

She shook her head. She hadn't known there was a St Lucy, and that there ever had been did not come into things now. 'Come with me,' she had made him say, knowing that it was fantasy. 'Come with me,' and he talked to her then about Scandinavia, as now he did about his childhood past. And she stole away from the farmhouse, closing the door on the quietened kitchen, the unlaid table, no saucepans simmering on the stove. People would hear that she wasn't there, the Corrigans and Gahagan, the shop people in Rathmoye, Mrs Hadden, Miss Connulty, the priests, the Cloonhill nuns. It frightened her to hear herself reviled, but when she heard it often it might not any more.

He took the postcard from her and put it back on the windowsill.

'I'm sorry there's no cake.' He poured the tea he'd made. He had remembered jam – raspberry from the half-and-half, he explained. He said the bread was fresh.

'I don't need anything,' she said, but she ate the bread he'd cut because he'd cut it, and drank the tea he'd poured. And afterwards, in the drawing-room, he told her how the room had been, describing the furniture that was no longer there. He prised out the drawing-pins that held in place a row of pictures on a wall. Each time smoothing the wrinkled paper, he handed one and then another to her.

'Their watercolours are what's left of my mother and my father,' he said.

He said he had known the name of the strand where

people were having a picnic, but had forgotten it. The couple who conversed in an empty theatre were actors who'd been famous in their day. It was at the corner of a Dublin street that the three-card trick was played on an umbrella, the tulip tree was in a Dublin garden. 'She used to come here,' he said about a girl in an ivory-white dress who was stretched out on the upturned boat by the lake, her long legs languidly spread, a red scarf knotted at her throat.

'Have them,' he said. 'Please have them.'

She shook her head. To accept what she was offered was to say that she would stay and he would go, that the giving and the taking were the gesture of parting, and parting's confirmation. As once she would not have, she knew to say no.

She was not pressed and soon afterwards she rode back to Rathmoye. She had meat to get in Hearn's, and a few groceries in the Cash and Carry. Then she looked up Scandinavia in Hogan's, where she had once bought a new exercise-book for the accounts. School books were kept too, and she found Scandinavia in an atlas. When she saw its shape, one side of it jagged, she remembered the glossy map draped over the blackboard. A book she took from the shelves said that Norway's fjords probed deeply inland, that forest and water and coastal archipelagos gave Sweden its brooding nature. 'Denmark's the little one,' she remembered the geography nun saying, and she remembered the mermaid on the rock.

Different languages, not many cities, the book said. Corn was grown. Iron ore was mined at Kiruna. Place names were unpronounceable. *Gudbrandsdalen*, Ellie read,

Henne Strand, Sundsfjord, Kittelfjäll. But easier to say, there were *Gothenburg* and *Malmö* too, *Leksand, Finse.*

The Vikings were of Scandinavia. Neatly in chalk on the blackboard, that came back to her. Sister Agnes the geography nun had been.

23

Orpen Wren went about the shops. He waited at the railway station. He sat down in the Square, trying to remember who it was he had to see, who it was he had to pass on a message to. The Rakes of Mallow: that came back to him, that being said in the library, but he didn't know why it came back now. 'The Rakes of Mallow aren't in it.' Her voice faltered when she said it, as any mother's voice would, and then she cried. Was her son dead in Portumna? she asked Mr Boyle and Mr Boyle said only lamed and she said thank God. The coachman the whole time was silent.

Twilight, then darkness, spread through what Orpen Wren recalled: a thickening fog, sound and faces distorted, then lost. It would lift, today some time, tomorrow. Or maybe it wouldn't.

The papers were back. The woman had arranged for the coal delivery. The first fires would be lit, you'd hear the pianos played. You'd hear the horses whinnying in the yard, you'd hear the dogs, you'd hear the voices. 'We'll go,' the master said from his bed.

Thomas John Kinsella, was the memorial inscription on the pedestal. *Died for Ireland, 1776–1798.* There was more, the letters small, incised; but the name and the dates were enough. Orpen looked up at the young, bony features, the open shirt and bare forearms, and felt sorry for the hero who had died so early in his life. He often said he was sorry when he sat here in the Square, enjoying the company. He was fond of Thomas Kinsella.

He went again to the railway station. He bought a tin of soup in the corner shop in Hurley Lane. He watched the children at hopscotch.

Thomas John Kinsella, he read again when he returned to the Square. He slept for a while and when he woke it was because he was wagging his head, reproving himself for having forgotten what he now remembered: whom it was he had to see and give a message to.

He set off at once, but after a while the distance seemed too far and he knew he'd have to wait for a better day.

24

Dillahan dismantled the corral he erected every year for the shearing. As always at this busy time, he had put off the dismantling for longer than he'd intended. Weeks had passed and every day he'd told himself that the sprawl of old gates and corrugated iron was unsightly, the garish red binding twine, the swirls of wool scattered.

Ellie gathered the lengths of twine when they were released, pulling apart the knots in them. She raked up the wool, combing it out of the grass. She had brought the fertilizer bag from last year to take it away in.

'Better we'd get it done early next time,' her husband said while he stacked the rusting gates on the trailer.

There was withering all around them: of the nettles that had earlier been verdant in the hedges, of drooping foxgloves and cow-parsley. Hard, dry earth was exposed where sheep had congregated, grass was yellowing. But the September air was cool and fresh, pleasanter than August's brashness.

Ellie hardly noticed all this, but knew from other years that it was there. She tried to think of that, of the first time she had raked up the wool, and getting to know this field; of the first time she'd collected the eggs in the crab-apple orchard, and seeing the hares at night. But Shelhanagh House kept breaking into what she imposed – its shabby, deserted rooms, the tennis court, the quiet old dog resting on the grass, the postcard of St Lucy. And Scandinavia broke in too; and she was there, in its strangeness.

'Well, it kept fine for us still,' her husband said. 'I don't know did we ever have a dryness like it. Good girl,' he complimented her, a note of sympathy in his tone, for her task was tedious.

He started the tractor and she heard the clatter of the trailer's load until it began to fade and then was gone. She tied the lengths of binding twine into a bundle and put it to one side. She filled the fertilizer bag with the pile of wool she'd made. She was all morning in the field.

*

The small churchyard was shadowy with a twilight of its own, overhung with maple trees and oaks, its dark yews like sentinels among them, old headstones crooked or fallen. How random the chance of circumstance was, Florian reflected, surveying the grass that had grown high on the mound that was his parents' grave. How much of chance it was that Natalia Verdecchia, a child of Genoa, should be here now because she had loved a *soldato di ventura*. The two names were sharply incised on unpolished limestone, the letterer who had been commissioned chosen for the sensitivity of his touch. All that had mattered – that they should be together, that skill and quality should mark their place in a graveyard, as their devotion to one another and the gift they'd shared had marked their lives. It wasn't easy to believe that they lay in silence, together yet out of touch.

A man was working with a hoe on the gravel paths and Florian borrowed a pair of shears from him. He cut the grass on the grave, pulled out brambles that hadn't yet established themselves. The day before he died his father had apologized for what might have seemed to be shared also: disappointment in an only child. He was insistent that there had never been that, and Florian had pretended too.

He returned the shears, and wandered among the graves before he went back to the one he'd tidied. How well they had loved! he reflected, tracing with a finger the two names on the gravestone. How well they had known how to live, how little they'd been a nuisance in other people's lives. He hoped it would be difficult to forget Ellie Dillahan, that at least there would be that.

He had left his bicycle at the lich-gate. The chain had begun to slip and he took it to be tightened, since he intended to cycle all the way to Dublin when he left. All night it would take if he set out in the evening. 'Never leave your bicycle on a street in Dublin,' his father used to say, but he would do that, leaving it for anyone.

He called in at the office of the solicitors who had drawn up the conveyance for the sale of Shelhangh House. He requested that what money was owed to him after the numerous deductions were made should be lodged with the Castledrummond branch of the Bank of Ireland. He made arrangements at the bank regarding the availability to him of such funds as soon as he was abroad. He bought a bicycle lamp; he hadn't possessed one before.

*

Ellie picked out clothes and put them ready, folded, in one side of a drawer. She bought in food: tins so that there would be something in the house, Three Counties cheese, a cut of bacon that would keep. It was only right that there should be food enough for a while, and a store of tins was always useful anyway.

The zip of the red holdall she had taken to Lahinch years ago was jammed and she couldn't free it. She had bought it in the second-hand shop and that the zip kept sticking hadn't mattered then, but it mattered now and she looked in Corbally's to see what was on offer. She didn't buy anything, knowing she could come back for one of the holdalls she was shown. She would get in a few more tins when that time came, and vegetables that would keep for a while. She would put out rashers and put out eggs so that there'd be something easy for him at first. She was not unaware that in doing so she was anticipating too much, that what had begun as fantasy was every day acquiring a little more of reality. She tried to prevent herself from allowing this, but couldn't.

25

The waitress at Olery was talkative. She stood with the checked cloth she always carried with her for wiping the tables. You wouldn't know where the time went to, she said. Since Easter she'd been at the tearooms and you wouldn't credit the days going by. A few weeks and she'd be starting her winter job, back in Dublin, where she came from. The Log Cabin, Phibsborough: Leitrim Street, she'd done a winter there before.

'If ever you'd be passing,' she invited.

Florian nodded. He had smiled now and then while listening to what they were being told. Ellie was quiet, in a navy-blue anorak he hadn't seen before.

'I'll bring your teas,' the waitress said, and added that she was a Phibsborough girl herself. 'I got to know you these past few months,' she said before she went away.

Theirs was the only table occupied in the tearooms. Outside a man with an electric hedge-trimmer was clipping the maze, the flex trailing behind him. They'd noticed as they passed it, a sign saying that the maze was closed today. They could hear the hum of the trimmer from where they were.

Two elderly women came in, continuing a conversation. Florian watched them while they sat down, and while they changed their minds and went to another table, giggling a bit.

'But, Ellie,' he began to say, reverting to what had been interrupted by the waitress talking about herself. 'Ellie –'

'I would go with you. To anywhere.'

The pleasant sound of quietened laughter came from the table where the two women, amusing one another, conversed again. Their tea, a lot of it, was spread out on a paper tablecloth and the waitress with her empty tray flat beneath one arm answered questions about what the scones and iced cakes contained, for it seemed that there were diets to consider.

Florian listened, reluctant to engage in what was being pressed upon him. Alone in the newness of somewhere, he knew now he would exploit imagination's ragged bits and pieces, tease order out of formless nothings, begin again and then again: how could he say it? That in some small quiet town he would take a room and work, and safely from afar try not to love, for ever, Isabella? How could he say a single word of such confessing when instead he could make a decent lie of the unpitying, unforgiving truth: would it have cost too much to say, or ever to have said, 'I love you'?

The waitress came again and, surmising something in the silence as she approached, only wrote out her bill and left it on the table.

'We've had our summer, Ellie.'

He said it softly, as gently as he could, rejecting falsity, for time would contradict it, add injury to injury, and pain to pain, and shame to shame. Time's searching wisdom would punish both of them, and punish ruthlessly.

They began to go. At the door more people were coming in and they stood back to let them pass.

'Without you there is nothing,' Ellie said.

The man was taking down the sign about the maze being closed, his long electric flex coiled up. He nodded to them, knowing them as the waitress did.

*

Clumps of rush had begun to grow and Dillahan knew that the ground in this corner was waterlogged. Broken or clogged land-drains, it would be, more likely broken. He advanced a yard or so further and was in a marsh. But that was all that was wrong with Gahagan's field, except for the fencing and general neglect, and he had suspected trouble in this corner. He could guess where the drain ran, a single pipe he imagined: he'd be able to dig it out himself. He'd done well out of the purchase, and he knew he had.

He walked around the boundary, rabbit-burrowing everywhere, the worst year for rabbits he'd ever known. He would replace the old wooden gate with an iron one, and the trough while he was at it. There was a dead elm in the road hedge and he was sizing it up, wondering if he could fell it himself, when he heard a bicycle beyond the bend and then Ellie went by. He thought she'd see him there, but she didn't. He called after her, wanting to show her the marshy corner, but she rode on, not hearing him.

26

No note invited her again to Shelhanagh House. He did not come when she waited at the gate-lodge ruins, where in the beginning so many times he had waited himself. The piece of iron with which he'd dug the ivy out was still on the grass where he had left it.

Ellie went away, returned later that same day. Had he gone already, the formalities completed sooner than the date? Was he there now, in Henne Strand or Finse or Malmö? Was his house already made different with other people's furniture?

Again she left the gate-lodge ruins, again returned.

*

Jessie wasn't there, waking up in the open doorway when Florian did. She wasn't in the kitchen, and he looked for her in the garden and then walked to the lake, calling her. He was still in his pyjamas, which had become sodden where they trailed through the long grass. He searched the garden again, and then went back to the house, to the sculleries and the unused dining-room, the drawing-room, and what had once been his darkroom. In one of the empty attics, huddled into a corner, she tried to wag her tail at him.

'Poor Jess,' he murmured.

He warmed milk in the kitchen and took it back to her but she didn't want it. He cradled her in his arms but she

173

struggled slightly and kept slipping away. He put her down in the place she'd chosen and crouched beside her.

'Poor Jess,' he said again, and she made another effort to move her tail, to thump the floor the way she knew she should. An eye regarded him, demanded nothing, trusting features that had always been trusted. Her tongue lolled tiredly out. She tried to pant. A few minutes later she died.

He dug her grave in a corner where she used to lie when the sun was too hot, or in spring, watching for rabbits. She had been fetched from somewhere a couple of miles away, the last one in a litter. His father had walked there, returning with the small bundle in his arms. 'Peko,' his father had suggested. 'Jessie,' his mother said.

Florian carried her downstairs, through the kitchen to the garden. He sat on the grass, his arms around her, her body stiffening, still warm. Then he buried her.

Afterwards, in the house, he sensed an eeriness, as if it had been waiting for this particular departure, another in an exodus that was now almost complete. He found it hard to settle and walked to Greenane Crossroads to leave the key of the hall door with Mrs Carley a day early.

'They'll find the others in an empty polish tin in the kitchen,' he said. 'If you could tell them I'll leave that tin in one of the cupboards.'

'I will of course.'

'Jessie died this morning.'

'Ah, the dear help poor Jessie!'

'I was going to ask you if you'd have her. For the bit of time left to her.'

'Of course I would have. Of course.'

'Otherwise –'

'I know, I know.'

They were in the licensed half of the premises and Mrs Carley, on hearing the news, had at once poured Florian a glass of whiskey.

'You couldn't but like that dog,' she said, replacing the bottle on the shelf. 'Nor the Kilderrys either. We'll miss the style of the Kilderrys hereabouts.'

Mrs Carley's plump presence, full of goodwill and fondness for the human race, hadn't changed in the years Florian had known her. She'd been the last of the maids at Shelhanagh before she married into the half-and-half, and it had never been a source of resentment that her wages were often delayed until another picture was sold. She came back later to preside over tea after both funerals – a huge spread supplied by herself, for a small gathering on each occasion.

Florian stayed, talking about the snow that came unexpectedly and lay on the ground for so long in the winter of nineteen forty-six, about being spared the war, about times he hardly remembered.

'You'll be all right, will you?' Suddenly, almost sharply, there was concern in Mrs Carley's easygoing tone.

'I will. Of course I will.'

'You're young to go wandering all the same.'

The talk changed again, slipping back into the past, which was Mrs Carley's favourite conversational period. She had been remembered as Nellie at Shelhanagh, but her time there had for the most part been before Florian's and he considered the formality of her married name to be her due: he had always called her Mrs Carley.

'They'll pull it together again,' he said, referring to the couple who had bought the house.

Someone came into the grocery as he was speaking and Mrs Carley held her hand out, across the counter.

'God bless,' she said.

*

Ellie waited when she had pulled the bell-chain a couple of times, then she went in. The hall door hadn't been locked when she'd come before and it wasn't now.

She called out, but she could tell he wasn't there. She wheeled her bicycle into the yard. The back door, too, was open.

She walked about the house. Upstairs, she found his bed unmade and made it. An empty suitcase was open on the floor, waiting to be packed. His passport was on the mantelpiece.

In the drawing-room the rickety table was gone, but the pictures he had wanted her to have were still in the pile he'd made of them, on the floor now. The book he'd told her about finding was in the kitchen, on the table, but she didn't open it.

She washed the dishes in the sink, then took a chair out to the yard. His dog must have gone with him, she thought, wondering where that was.

*

When Florian returned from Greenane he noticed that one of the two remaining chairs was no longer in the kitchen. He couldn't remember taking it somewhere else and then he saw the washed dishes on the draining-board. From the window he saw Ellie in the yard.

'I'm sorry,' she said when he told her Jessie had died.

176

Thrown up by his digging, a scattering of clay had not yet dried on the grass. A blackbird flew away when they went there.

'I thought your neighbours' harvesting . . .' Florian began to say.

Ellie shook her head. All that was over, she said.

'I couldn't not come. I couldn't.'

'You've been crying, Ellie.'

'I thought you'd gone. I could see that wasn't the way of it but even so in the quiet I thought you'd gone.'

'Well, I haven't. I'm here.'

And there was still all day, Florian said, and all day tomorrow. He put his arms around her. She said she couldn't bear to think about tomorrow.

'Ellie . . .'

'Please,' she whispered. 'Please. I've come to you.'

27

He was tired. He had met no one on the roads for a long time, no one to ask, no signposts because the roads were small. It wasn't right where he was now. He felt it wasn't and he asked in a house he came to, a dark, cement house among trees.

'I know you,' the child who opened the door greeted him, and he said he had walked out from Rathmoye, that his name was Orpen Wren.

'Sometimes I'd forget it. When you get old it isn't easy.'

'It's just I saw you a few times,' the child said. 'When we'd be Rathmoye I'd see you.'

Orpen asked for directions. He wasn't going further, he said. He'd go back now to Rathmoye if he could discover the way. It was the third time he'd come looking for the destination he couldn't find, but he didn't say that.

'There's no one here only me,' the child said. 'They're out at work.'

He had thought the child was a boy, but he saw now she was a girl wearing trousers. Her hair was cut short, but no shorter than many a boy's. Her eyes were a light shade of blue.

'Are you not in a car?' she asked.

'I never had a car.'

'It's a good step in to Rathmoye.'

'I walked all Ireland once. Am I near Lisquin?'

'Ah, no, you're not.'

'It isn't Lisquin I'm after. It's only I know my bearings from Lisquin. It's a man I came looking for.'

'Go down the road till you'll come to a black-tarred gate. Keep on past the gate till you'll come to a four-crossroads. Go to your left and go right at the sharp corner. You'll get on to the big road then and Rathmoye's marked up on the signpost. Will I tell you again?'

Orpen requested that, and then thanked the child. He found the black gate but when he went on he couldn't remember the rest of the directions and would have been lost again if a woman on a bicycle hadn't walked with him to the crossroads.

'Who were you looking for out this way?' she asked him and said he had strayed by a fair step when he told her.

She drew a map on a piece of brown paper she tore off a parcel. 'That's the best way you'll do it from Rathmoye,' she said. 'Don't lose it now for another day.'

He rested after she left him, sitting on the grass verge. Then he went on, put right again by tinkers on the side of the road.

28

When Ellie woke up she didn't know where she was, and then remembered. She heard a car. Coming into the room, Florian said:

'The men to tow away the Morris Cowley.'

She asked him what time it was. He said half past twelve, or nearly.

'Have they gone, the men?'

'They're going now.'

She closed her eyes, not wanting to be awake. He was in his shirtsleeves, his tweed waistcoat unbuttoned. He was looking down at her.

'Don't be upset,' he said.

Sunlight made a pattern with the shadows on the boards of the floor and on her clothes where she had thrown them, her bangle, and the ring she had taken from her finger. Her blue dress was crumpled. One shoe was on its side.

'I'll make tea,' he said.

When he went downstairs she found a bathroom in a part of the house she hadn't been in before. It was a bathroom that wasn't used, the small bath chipped and stained, grit fallen into it from the ceiling. But water came when she turned on the single tap at the wash-basin and she bathed her face.

The water was cold. There were no towels. There wasn't

soap. A cloth had hardened into a bundle on the window-sill and she ran water over it, and washed herself.

She didn't hurry. She didn't want tea, she wanted to be alone. A pool gathered on the floor while she washed and she tried to soak it up with the cloth.

A nun had gone to a man at the sawmills in Templeross. Sometimes she was called Roseline after the Blessed Roseline, but that was always known to be made up, for the nun was nameless at Cloonhill, mistily there in whispered tales passed down through generations. The man would come delivering logs in winter and she went to him, her habit folded on her bed, her crucifix, her beads, her missal, her shoes left too. All that was said, although it was forbidden to say anything.

Wondering what to dry herself with, Ellie sat on the edge of the bath. In the round, discoloured mirror above the basin there were glimpses of her nakedness when she moved. She never liked not having clothes on and she looked away. She was cold.

A few said the man wasn't there when the nun went to him, that she searched for him on the streets of cities, that he was never there again. Some said she begged on the streets and was known to have been a nun. Some said that when she was old she was found in the river at Limerick.

The bolt of the door wouldn't move at first but did when Ellie tried again. She listened and could hear nothing, not footsteps, not voices. Then she heard the car being towed away.

In the bedroom she dried herself on a sheet she pulled off the bed. *Éire, Ireland, Irelande*, it said on the passport that was displayed as the postcard of the saint was in the kitchen, more gilded letters bright on its green cover: *Pas, Passport, Passeport*.

She put her ring on again when she was dressed, secured the clasp of her bangle, tidied her hair as best she could with her fingers because her comb was in her handbag in the hall. A pigeon was murmuring outside the open window and then she heard the rattle of the garage doors being closed. She hung the sheet to dry on hooks that were there for a curtain-rail. She pulled the bedclothes off to air the bed. She didn't want to go downstairs and didn't go when he called, but when he called again she went.

*

'Stay a bit longer,' Florian said, and the hall-door bell jangled as he spoke.

He poured two cups of tea before he went to answer it. 'Forgotten something,' he said.

It was a wrench, put down somewhere when a bolt on the Morris Cowley had had to be tightened. He helped the two men to look for it and found it in the yard by the garage doors.

'Devil take it,' the man he returned it to said. 'That thing could hide itself in your flannel and you wouldn't know.'

*

He was carrying the chair she'd taken to the yard when he came back. He said it was a tool they had left behind.

Better just to go, she thought, but still she didn't. 'Things end,' he'd said the day he told her everything, and she had understood and for a while accepted that.

He had put his tie on, his jacket. A little of her tea had spilt on to the saucer and he wiped it away with a cloth.

'I'm sorry.' She whispered, not hearing herself, not knowing what she was apologizing for, then knowing it was for everything. For being a bother with her regrets that weren't regrets, for her longings and her tears, because she had no courage, because she had come today and made it all worse.

'I'm sorry too,' he said. 'I let things happen. I notice them too late.'

She shook her head. She sipped the tea he'd poured. It had no taste.

'I have that way with me,' he said. 'I'm reticent when I shouldn't be.'

The doors of the wall-cupboards were hanging open, yellowing green, as the walls themselves were. There was nothing on the shelves, nothing on the row of hooks above them. The saucepans and china stacked on the floor, the two chairs, the table and what was on it were what was left in the kitchen now.

Better to go, Ellie thought again, and again did not.

'There was a nun we'd talk about,' she said.

*

The bleak recounting of events affected Florian as he listened. It chilled him, but a nun torn from her vows by passion's torment, and wretched years later her body floating on the water, did not seem to belong, had no place, surely, in a passing summer friendship, even though love came into it, too.

'I thought of her,' Ellie said. 'It's only that.'

'You're not a nun, Ellie. It's different. All of it is different.'

'Sometimes a girl would say the nun deserved her fate. Sometimes a girl would cry, and another girl would tell us to be reminded of the nun's suffering whenever we saw logs blazing. The log man he was called.'

'Ellie –'

'How is it different? How is it, though?'

About to answer, Florian hesitated, and then said nothing. Did she understand more than he did because the pain was hers, not his? Accepting the burden of perfect faith, a novice had promised more than she could give; a man delivering firewood lured her from her knees because he liked the look of her. Could there really be an echo of that nun's misery long ago in what so ordinarily had come about this summer and now must end? Was despair, with all its bitterness, governed less by misfortune's content than by some law of its own?

'When will you go tomorrow?'

The suddenness of the question, the change of mood, startled Florian and for a moment he didn't know what he'd been asked. When it was repeated he said he would ride through the night to Dublin, that that was how he'd always wanted to go.

'Come tomorrow, Ellie. At least to say goodbye.'

She did not immediately respond either. When she did it was to say it would be too much to be with him on the day he went away.

'I could not.'

Florian sensed the truth of that: it was in her manner, and he heard it in her measured intonation. It was a wince in her face while she spoke, it was in the turn of her head when she looked away from him.

'I could not,' she said again, out of a silence.

*

They sat for longer at the table, the cigarette Florian had put out to smoke unsmoked, the tea he'd made gone cold. This was what he would take with him, he thought. This was what he would leave behind. Tidily laid out, these moments now would haunt whole days.

He had pitied the infant left in a corner of some yard or on a convent step, had pitied the child given a place among the unwanted, the girl who had become a servant. Her loneliness had been his when they were friends – before, too greedily, he asked too much of friendship, and carelessly allowed a treacherous love to flourish. She had come to him, and pity now was nourished by his greater guilt, and guilt was lent some part of pity's dignity. A wild delusion seemed – because of what today had happened – to be less wild, a hopeless yearning less intolerant of reason. They sat not speaking, and time seemed not to pass.

*

The silence held. But when they walked in the garden their choked conversation flickered into life again. The lobelia, the buddleia, the last of the smoke tree's summer mist, berberis, garrya, mahonia: Ellie learnt the names, she had not known them. And they went to the lake to see if the summer bird had come back, but still it hadn't. And then, beyond the plum trees, where there'd been raspberries before, they spoke of Scandinavia.

Dillahan turned off the ignition of the tractor because he hadn't been able to hear what the man said.

'What d'you want?' he asked again.

The man had come from nowhere. A moment before he appeared he hadn't seemed to be there. He didn't reply to what he'd been asked, and Dillahan looked more closely at him. He must have come out of the field that had been Gahagan's. Then he realized the man was Orpen Wren.

'Is it Mr Dillahan, sir?'

'I'm Dillahan.'

'I know you, sir. I know you well.'

'Yes.'

'It's not often I'm as far abroad as this, sir. It's not often I stray away from the town. You know where you are within a town, sir.'

'What d'you want?'

'No more than a word, sir,' Orpen Wren said. 'No more than that, sir.'

'Oh, we do, we do,' the salesman said. 'Wait now till I'll get a few out for you.'

He was an older man, his back a little humped, starched white collar and cuffs, a shop assistant's dark suit. Ellie hadn't seen him in Corbally's before. There hadn't been anyone in the luggage department when she'd looked at the holdalls a week or so ago.

'Bear with me a minute,' he said now.

In the garden it had felt like a dream and it still did when she went back to the house for her handbag. He wheeled her bicycle out of the yard, over the gravel at the front, on to the road. He was waiting for her there and she mentioned the jammed zip of the holdall and he said get a new one. She couldn't remember if she had looked round when she rode away, but if she had she retained no image of his standing there alone. She remembered noticing the Dano Mahoney as she went by it. There'd been the sign for Rathmoye, in Irish and in English, and then the Ford advertisement and the one for Raleigh Bicycles, and the request to go slowly. 'Be sure, Ellie. Be certain,' was what he'd said when they stood on the road. No more than that except to say to get a holdall.

'We have this fellow.' The salesman was opening one of the suitcases he'd brought. 'In a two-tone or the blue,' he said.

She had asked for a holdall, and described again what she wanted – something that would fold in on itself when it wasn't in use, something that could be attached to the carrier of a bicycle. She didn't explain further, she didn't go into details.

'Well, I'd say we have that.' The salesman went away again and returned with two holdalls. He unzipped them on the counter, drawing attention to inside pockets. 'We have it green. Or a tan with a Rexine trim.'

She wondered if he knew her, or if he'd ask after she'd gone and be told who she was by Miss Burke or the man she bought dress material from. She wondered if they'd talk about it, how she'd bought a holdall, where she was going.

'I'd rather the green,' she said.

'That's a better bag than the Rexine,' the man said. 'The Rexine finish hasn't the appeal it had one time.'

'Would you be able to parcel it up for me?'

'I would, of course. Would I clip off the price tag while I'm at it?'

'It doesn't matter.'

'The latest thing is you have an expansion possibility on the bigger size of suitcase. We have one or two of that type of thing if you'd find the holdall wouldn't be spacious enough.'

She said she thought it would be and asked if she could have extra string to tie the parcel on to her bicycle.

'Of course you could.'

He gave her more string than she needed, saying it would come in useful. He asked her if she'd be going to the circus and she said she doubted it. He loved a circus, he said.

'Drop in on me next time you'll be in the shop,' he said, 'till I'd know was it a satisfactory container for you.'

It had still felt a dream all the time she was riding away from Shelhanagh House. It still did now, a salesman who was a stranger to her talking about a circus and bringing her suitcases instead of a holdall, giving her half a ball of string when she asked for just a little.

The Square looked different when she turned into it. It wasn't crowded, but a lorry was delivering pavement kerbing in Magennis Street, holding everything up. She wheeled her bicycle around it, where people walking were going.

Miss Connulty must have greeted her. She must have said something because she nodded as if she had. And something was missing when so suddenly she whispered that love was a madness.

A restraining hand was on the handlebars of Ellie's bicycle, and Miss Connulty smiled a little, as if to soften what might have sounded abrupt. The lorry slowly began to move. Standing aside for two other women who were going by, Miss Connulty said nothing else.

Dillahan tried to make sense of it. He sat on the tractor in the yard, and after a time the sheepdogs slouched away as if influenced by his brooding. He went through it all again, every word that had been spoken, even by himself, his interruptions, his efforts to lead the conversation into areas that might be fertile enough to nurture reality in the morass of confusion. He went back, in his thoughts, to other times, searching them in turn for a connection with what had been said, threading fact and fantasy and finding in their conjunction the blemished truth. For everything was blemished in the talk there'd been, and at its best the truth itself might also be.

He climbed down from the tractor seat and slowly walked across the yard to the back door of the farmhouse, his gait affected by the disquiet he took with him. The sheepdogs stayed where they were, their noses stretched forward, resting on the backs of their paws.

It was late afternoon, just before five, when Ellie arrived back at the farmhouse with what she'd bought – tins of corned beef as well as the green holdall. As she rode into the yard she saw the tractor there and was surprised. It was parked untidily, crookedly, in the way other vehicles that came into the yard sometimes were. She remembered he'd said he intended to plough the sixteen acres where he'd had a crop of rape this year, and he had a couple of jobs to do if he'd be able to get down to them. He said he'd come in for something to eat between twelve and half past, and she had left out cold meat. He couldn't, surely, be still here, she thought, and he couldn't have finished the sixteen acres already. She wondered if the tractor was giving trouble. When the dogs didn't come to her she knew something was wrong.

The house was silent, as if he wasn't there. But she knew he was, because the dogs were in the yard. She didn't put her bicycle away. She undid the knots of the string that held the parcel in place on her carrier, grappling with them where she'd made them too tight, forcing the parcel loose when she couldn't undo the last one. She pushed open the door of one of the sheds. There was a pile of tarpaulins in a corner. As best she could, she concealed the holdall among them.

She left her bicycle where it was, slipping from the

handlebars the carrier bags that contained the tins she'd bought. She didn't want to go into the house. For a moment she saw the sunlight dappling the boards of the floor, her dress where she had thrown it down, one of her shoes on its side; she heard her own voice asking if the men who'd come had gone. As soon as he saw her he would know, somehow he would. About today, about every day.

She lifted the back-door latch, but something obstructed the door, preventing it from opening as freely as it always did. He would be lying there, the gun he went after the pigeons with when they raided his crops beside him. There'd been a farmer took his life near Donaghmore and they'd prayed for him at Cloonhill. A man who couldn't right himself after his wife died, Sister Mary Frances had said, a man she'd known. And another farmer not long ago, gone bankrupt in east Kerry, found hanged. But the obstruction at the door was only a wellington boot fallen over.

'What is it?' she asked, not wanting to be told.

He was sitting in front of the stove. He had pulled the dampers out although it wasn't cold today. The plate of meat was where she'd left it on the table, a mesh dome keeping the flies off, the knife and fork where she'd laid them, the bread still wrapped in a tea-towel, the butter covered, the teapot ready for his tea when he made it.

'What is it?' she asked again.

He didn't turn round. He was hunched, his hands pressed together.

'What's troubling the dogs?' she asked.

He turned his head then. He'd upset the dogs, he said.

Being upset himself, he had brought that on. They'd been confused: he'd go and settle them.

'Why are you upset?'

He didn't answer, as if he hadn't heard, or as if it was too much to say. He went to the yard and she heard the tractor started. The kitchen door was open, but she didn't have to look. He was a tidy man even in distress: the tractor was being driven to where it should be. She heard his voice with the dogs, then he came in again.

'He was talking to me on the road,' he said. 'Old Orpen Wren.'

A coldness came in her stomach, her arms felt weak. Orpen Wren wasn't sane, you couldn't understand what he was on about. Nobody gave credence to his wild assertions, to his talk about people who were dead; nobody took Orpen Wren seriously. But the chilly feeling was still there, and she willed it in her thoughts that Miss Connulty would not be mentioned also, or someone else whom gossip had reached, someone she didn't know about. Frantically in a hurry, her snatched words tumbled about, her silent plea made formless, no more than an expression of fear.

'He talks to everyone.' She heard her voice as if it came from somewhere else, as if she were not there, as if this were not happening. She tried to pray that it was not, but the words still wouldn't come properly.

'I was upset, what he said to me.'

She tried not to hear. She wanted time to go on, emptily to accumulate. She carried the shopping she'd done for him into the scullery, although not everything she'd bought belonged there. He didn't call her back. He sat where he'd been sitting before and when she returned to the kitchen he spoke again, but she didn't hear at first and he repeated what he'd said. Orpen Wren had held his hand up for him to stop and he had. He said that sometimes you used to see him on the road beyond the town; but that was long ago.

'I thought he'd got himself lost,' he said.

He didn't go on, as if there was nothing else to say. He stared at the floor, hunched again, his hands together as they had been before. He was so different he seemed a stranger to her and she knew she was to blame for that, not he.

'You've had nothing to eat,' she said. 'I left the meat out for you.'

'I couldn't take it.'

'Were you here since the morning?'

'Ten to twelve I came in. About that.'

'I'll make something for us. That meat will keep.'

She turned away, with the knife and fork she was about to lay as a second place in her hand. She didn't look at her husband, frightened because of what might be in her eyes. He said:

'Is it put about I could see her behind the trailer? Is it put about that I couldn't see she had the child in her arms?'

'What?' There was only relief in her single, startled ejaculation, hardly even a question in it, hardly even the word itself. 'What're you talking about?'

'Sometimes at Mass I'd know people would be looking at me.'

'Of course they're not.'

'Is it they're saying in Rathmoye she was going with one of the St Johns?'

'Of course they aren't saying that. Why would they be?'

'He was on about the St Johns going with any handy woman they'd find.'

'When the accident happened in the yard the St Johns were gone from here. They were ages gone then.'

'There's one came back. He saw her with him. A few times he saw the two of them. The old trouble, he called it.'

'He says anything. It's different every time what he says. There's no sense to it. He hasn't sense left in him.'

'He was sorry for me on account of the child. It was for that he stopped me on the road. A St John came back, Ellie, the time I was careless with the tractor in my own yard.'

'There's nowhere to come back to. These thirty years, there never was.'

'I didn't know it that a St John came back. Only myself didn't know it. He's saying no more than what'd be said round about.'

'There's no talk like that in Rathmoye.'

'I hate going in there. Ever since the day I hated it.'

'Would a drop of whiskey do you good? Would I get the bottle from the scullery?'

'I used wonder would people be thinking I had whiskey taken the time I backed the trailer. Would they be saying I had drink in me? Would they be saying I shouldn't have backed with the sun in my eyes?'

'That isn't said at all.'

'Better it might be than what was said to me on the road.'

'Don't listen to his old rambling.'

'I never thought it'd be said what was said to me on the road.'

'You don't have to think it. It isn't true.'

'Did you hear it said yourself, Ellie? Did he say it to you the day I went for the loan and he was talking to you in the Square? Did other people say it to you? Is it that that has you troubled, Ellie?'

She said that no one had repeated a word of anything like it to her. All Orpen Wren ever talked about was the past, she said.

'It's the past has him in its grip, Ellie.'

'Yes, it is.'

'Coming out here, he was further than he ever is beyond the town. He told me that too. It was myself he was looking for, Ellie.'

'He talks to anyone.'

He shook his head as he stood up. He went to the scullery and came back with the whiskey bottle and a cup.

'I'm all right when I'm in the fields,' he said. 'Or when I'm with yourself in the house. It'd maybe be all right if I was walking in a town where no one'd know me.'

She watched him pouring out some of the whiskey that was kept to offer his relations when they came over from Shinrone once a year on a Sunday afternoon. She'd tasted it herself and hadn't liked it. She said again that people in Rathmoye weren't saying what he feared, that everything repeated to him today came out of a distorted mind, that Orpen Wren's rigmaroles were all his own. He shook his head.

'It takes a mad man to say it out.'

'It isn't true,' she said again.

'She came from better people than my own. But she never held it over me, she took me for what I was. I wouldn't have said she was a flighty woman, I wouldn't have said she was the kind to go with another man. But if she did who'd blame people for thinking what was said on the road? The age he is and everything, he walked the miles out to say he was sorry about the child. He said it wasn't good that he never said it before on account of he forgets things. The rest of it slipped out, the way it would when you haven't a grip on your wits. I always knew there was something. I always knew not to hold my head up in Rathmoye.'

He reached for the bottle on the floor beside where he sat. She thought he was going to pour more whiskey but he didn't. He said again a St John had come back the time he was careless with the tractor in his own yard. You couldn't blame people for what they'd think or what they'd say. You couldn't blame people for reaching a conclusion. You couldn't blame Orpen Wren.

'What he said to you is nothing only rubbish.'

Ellie hadn't sat down herself. All the time they'd been talking she had stood by the table with the knife and fork in her hand. She watched while he crossed the kitchen to return the whiskey bottle to the scullery shelves. He wasn't a drinking man: that had been discovered by the nuns and passed on to her before she'd come to the farm. He washed the cup out at the sink.

'I'll make us something to eat,' she said again.

She put the knife and fork down where she'd been

197

intending to. There was a numbness in her mind, all panic gone from it. Nothing happening there was what it felt like.

'He shook hands with me and then he went off,' her husband said.

He didn't want to eat, and nor did she. He went away and she heard the tractor again, before he drove it to the fields. In the silent kitchen it came coldly to her that the tragedy of the man who had taken her into his house was more awful by far than love's denial. It came like clarity in confusion, there was a certainty: it was too late. And it came coldly, too, that the truth she yet might tell to draw the sting of his agony would cause more suffering than she could inflict, more than any man who had done no wrong deserved.

33

Waking the next day, Florian was first of all aware that his dog was dead, and then the day before came jerkily back, like a film carelessly projected. He had woken to panic in the night, but afterwards had slept again and now was calmer. What was done was done, what would happen would happen. He washed and dressed, made coffee, heated milk. He hurried over nothing.

It was eight o'clock when a van came for the furniture and effects that had had to remain until now: his bed, his bedroom cupboard, two dressing-tables and a chest-of-drawers the new owners of Shelhanagh had said they'd like to have, then changed their minds about. The radio-gram should have gone earlier but there'd been a misun-derstanding and it hadn't. China was packed into a tea-chest, kitchenware into another. The skip would be there until evening, to take anything else.

The house was bleak, the emptiness complete when the men had gone, his footsteps the only sound. He prised Isabella's picture from the drawing-room wall. He com-pleted his packing of the small suitcase he hadn't used since his boarding-school days. On top of what clothes he was taking, in protective cardboard he placed the water-colours, his most valuable possession. A drawer had slipped out of the heavy kitchen table on its way to the furniture van, throwing on to the ground his father's waistcoat watch, his mother's only jewelled ring. He found a corner for them.

The pages of the *Fieldbook* had served their purpose and he relit his garden fire with them. He put away the spade he had used to dig the grave, beside other garden implements that by arrangement were to be left. In the yard he thought he heard a sound, coming from the garden, but there was no one there. At the lake he skimmed pebbles over the water and wondered if, anywhere, he would play this solitary game again.

He missed the rattling in the reeds, the fleeing of the water rats. He smoked a cigarette, leaning against the upturned boat, listening for bicycle wheels on the gravel.

*

Ellie left the house only to feed her hens and to retrieve the parcel from under the tarpaulins in the turf shed. She took the wrapping paper off and filled the green holdall with stones from the wall of the river-field, then watched it sinking into murky water.

It rained in the afternoon and Dillahan cut the winter's wood. In the shed he pulled out the boughs he had stacked, trimming them, chopping off brushwood with a hatchet. He had a couple of elm trunks, dead wood, dry as a bone. There was an oak bole he'd had for years.

The belts of the circular saw had slackened; the oil in the cogs was dry. He brushed out grime and sawdust, and his file on the teeth of the saw screeched when he sharpened them. He cleaned the spark plugs he had loosened. When he tried the engine it spluttered and then fired, with wisps of smoke and petrol fumes in the air.

He kept the engine turning over while he put away the

tools he had used – wire brush and spanners, the hammer he eased the motor clamp with, screwdriver, his oil can.

When the whine of the sawing began Ellie came out of the house, although he always said he could manage. She passed him each next length of wood, hardly any of them too heavy for her. All afternoon it took, the logs falling to a heap on the ground.

*

The skip swung a little in the air before it steadied and slowly descended to the lorry. The chains that had lifted it hung loose, and then were wound back into the crane. 'Good luck to you!' the driver called out before he drove away.

Florian had left himself without a book and, with nothing to do, he climbed up to the roof to look for the last time at the view it offered. He remembered being brought there the first time for the same purpose; and later, on his own, reading *Coral Island* there. Once Isabella and he had tried to sleep on the roof, but the lead which had been warm at first became cold and they had crept back into the house. And it was there, one summer after Isabella had gone back to Italy, that he first became addicted to the detective stories that were his mother's addiction all her life. Day after day in a heatwave he had read *The Fashion in Shrouds* and *The Crime at Black Dudley*, *Hangman's Holiday*, *Death and the Dancing Footman*.

From the roof the far-off mountains were unchanged, but the crowded summer fields were earthy now, empty and orderly and the same. Autumn was in the trees, bright berries of cotoneaster in the garden, busy squirrels.

He could see the road and would see her when she

came, but still she didn't and familiar guilt began, without a reason now. It faded while he waited, and on the way down through the house he went from room to room, closing the door of each behind him when he left it. At the bottom of the stairs a figure stood hesitantly in the gathering dusk. 'I came on in,' a man said, explaining then that he was here to read the electricity meter.

While this was being done and the electricity turned off, Florian again imagined he heard a sound outside; and listened, but it wasn't repeated. The bottle of champagne was still on the hall floor, ignored or forgotten by the front door. 'Would you like to have this?' he offered the meter-reader; and as if such generosity demanded that he should be sociable, the man stayed longer than he might have, relating anecdotes connected with houses changing hands. Some people took the lightbulbs when they went, he said.

*

'You made it easier for me,' Dillahan said, saying it suddenly when neither of them had spoken for a while. She had made it less frightening; for you could be frightened, he said, and not know why, only that fear had come from somewhere. You'd see that in an animal.

When the clocks changed next month he'd drive her over to Templeross, he said, and she wondered if, even after she'd been to confession, the nuns would know. Everything was calmer for a penitent, they used to say at Cloonhill, and she accepted that it was. But still she wondered if the nuns would see her as she used to be, or as she had become.

*

Twilight darkened in Shelhanagh House. Florian threw water on to the glow of his garden fire and stumbled about the empty kitchen. The tin he'd spoken about to Mrs Carley was already on a shelf in one of the wall-cupboards. He pulled over the shutters in the downstairs rooms. When he had locked the hall door from the outside he dropped the key through the letter-box and heard it fall on the flagstones. By the light of his bicycle lamp he strapped his suitcase on to the carrier.

*

That night Ellie didn't sleep. She hadn't slept the night before either. Not putting on the light she had got up and moved her clothes from the chair by the window and had sat there, looking out into the dark. She did so again, the window open a little as both of them liked it, the air chilly.

It was earlier now than when she'd sat there the night before, the last streaks of filmy moonlight slipping away from the yard below. It was a natural thing for a man who had accidentally killed his wife and child to dread suspicion. It was a natural thing that a tormented mind should be confused. In the single day that had passed Ellie had many times told herself all that; and told herself that if Miss Connulty asked her she would say the man she had been friendly with for a while had left Ireland. She would not deny that she'd been friendly with him. She would say his name and where he had lived.

At the window she began to feel cold, but still sat there. Tired as so often he was, her husband breathed heavily and was not restless. Everything had been easier for him since she came to his house, he had said this evening, everything better for him since she'd married him. There weren't many who would understand, he'd said.

Somewhere, far off, there was a light. She watched it moving, and knew. She put her clothes on and went downstairs quickly because the dogs would bark. She lifted a coat from one of the hooks on the back door. In the yard both dogs sleepily emerged to greet her.

She could hear nothing on the road. 'Come back,' she whispered, and the dog who'd been inclined to investigate obeyed. The other one hadn't moved from beside her.

The light was there again, coming out of the dip in the road, still far away. Sometimes one of the Corrigan boys went by on a bicycle at night, not often, and they never bothered with lights.

34

They walked away from the house, he pushing his bicycle, the sheepdogs with them.

'I thought he was dead,' she said.

She told him. There was a gun kept for rabbits and the pigeons. There had been silence everywhere, the tractor parked like that, the dogs morose. A farmer from near Donaghmore had taken his life, another farmer in east Kerry.

'All day today I tried to think of nothing,' she said.

*

They had not embraced. They did not now. He was a shadow beside her, little more than that.

'Why have you come?' she asked.

She felt him staring at her, trying to see her in the dark. When she asked again why he had come, he said because he wanted her to know that he had waited.

'I'll never forget being loved by you,' he said. 'Don't hate me, Ellie. Please don't hate me.'

*

He reached for her hand, but it wasn't there.

He would have destroyed her, he said. Not ever meaning to, he would have. He knew it, in the way of knowing something that couldn't be explained.

'People run away to be alone,' he said. Some people had to be alone.

'It isn't much of a goodbye,' he said.

He let a silence gather and so did she. There was a rustle in the undergrowth that might have been a fox's quick retreat. They paid it no attention.

'He saved you. That old man,' he said.

*

'It's cold.'

She turned away and he walked with her, still wheeling his bicycle. Any moment a light would go on in the house, she thought. Any moment her name would be called out, the back door thrown open. That mattered more than understanding. It mattered more than anything, was all that mattered.

She knew that this was so, yet still would have gone with him. She whispered, gathering the dogs to her.

'I couldn't hate you,' she said.

She didn't speak again, and nor did he.

*

He cycled slowly, the air raw on his face. The signpost to Crilly was lit up by his lamp as he went by. The road straightened, became a hill to freewheel down, and then the twists and turns began again. How useless being sorry was, and yet that, most of all, was what he felt, a soreness in him somewhere. Her grey-blue eyes had been no more than smudges in the dark.

*

She listened to the swish of wheels in motion before the sound dimmed away to nothing, before the flicker of light became faint and then was gone. The sheepdogs ambled into their shed. She crossed the yard, her footsteps light on the concrete surface. She lifted the latch of the door she had left unlocked, and closed the door behind her and softly turned the key.

In the kitchen she was guided by the votive gleam above the dresser. She took her shoes off and mounted the narrow stairs, each tread faintly creaking. The bedroom door was open, as she had left it too. She folded her clothes and laid them on the chair between the windows.

35

Orpen Wren slept. In Hurley Lane Bernadette O'Keeffe turned off a romantic drama and ended her day with a last long, slow nightcap. It was her happy time, when what she had was enough and enough was what she asked for. The cheques passed across the table, the letters signed, his putting to her this matter or that, his asking her what she thought, his acquiescent nod. Emotion, stalled, was not a nuisance in the night. The bright little screen, and night-caps, made a party of the room, its swaying furniture and uncertain floor, its garbled voices relieving Bernadette of a turmoil they themselves absorbed. That a beloved mother's death had failed to loosen a lifetime's iron bond did not in the cheerful night seem more than could be borne: so drowsy peace told Bernadette. And tomorrow – for it was not a dreaded Saturday or Sunday – there would be once more the papers fondly typed and carried to the quiet back bar, once more his commendation, once more their chat.

*

The Rathmoye street-lights had not yet been extinguished, but the streets themselves had emptied. The last of the public house stragglers had gone, the last of the lovers had parted. Two laundry women hurried away from their night work in Mill Street. Cats stalked the coal yards. Silently in the Square a mongrel dog ransacked a dustbin.

*

Drawing back the curtains of the big front room in readiness for the morning, Miss Connulty watched. The dog – yellowish, its tail cropped close – would be there again, since every night he came. But still she paused to watch, even though the house was full, which meant an early morning. A single shaft of light caught the bony features of Thomas John Kinsella, his gaping shirt, sleeves rolled up. That, too, at this late hour was never different.

Miss Connulty had begun to turn away from the window, about to go upstairs, when a movement that was not the dog's caught her eye. It alerted the dog too, who at once crept off, cringing, into the shadows. A man on a bicycle rode into the Square.

He was wearing the hat, there was a suitcase tied on to the bicycle's carrier. He didn't pause or dismount but went steadily on. Miss Connulty watched him turning out on to the Dublin road, and watched the dog returning to the dustbin. Soon after that the street-lights went out.

So all of it was over for Ellie Dillahan, Miss Connulty said to herself, all of it done with. Quietly ascending the stairs to the bathroom and her bedroom so as not to disturb the sleeping men around her, she remembered the closed sign pulled down over the glass of the chemist's door, and her father pouring the tea in the café of the Adelphi cinema. 'All done,' her father said. 'All over, girl.'

She washed, quietly running the tap. In her bedroom she undressed and Ellie Dillahan, coming again with her Friday eggs, confided in her; and Miss Connulty said if there's a child don't let anyone take the child away from you. Born as Dillahan's own since he believed it was, the child would make a family man of him again, and make the farmhouse different. And her own friendship with Ellie Dillahan would not be strained, now that the interloper who had ill-used her had at last shaken the dust of Rathmoye off his heels. The friendship would be closer, both of them knowing it could be, neither of them saying what should not be said and never would be.

Miss Connulty turned her bedside light off and a few moments later closed her eyes, though not in sleep. An infant child crawled towards her on the carpet of the big front room, and bricks were kept, and dolls or soldiers in the corner cupboard, rag books, a counting frame. The secret heart of Ellie Dillahan's life possessed the big front room, and later there were games of Snap and Ludo, and bagatelle, which as a child herself Miss Connulty had enjoyed. None of it was impossible.

36

On the streets of darkened towns, on roads that are often his alone, bright sudden moments pierce the dark: reality at second hand spreads in an emptiness.

Among the scattered tools, the nun stares up at nothing from where she lies. Girls close her eyes, although they are afraid. They brush away the sawdust from her habit and her shoes. They go to tell what they have found, then wash white-painted windows, gather wood. They sing in their heads a song they mustn't sing, and wonder who it is who doesn't want them. The windscreen wipers slush through rain, the man comes from the house and carries in the box. There is the place in the yard. There are the haunted days of June. She claims no virtue for her compassion, she does not blame a careless lover. She grows her vegetables, collects her eggs.

Horses canter in the breaking dawn, the open landscape fills, Old Kilmainham, Islandbridge. Seagulls rest on river walls, hops enrich the air.

The sea is calm, the engines' chug the only sound, the chill of autumn morning lingering. You know what you'll remember, he reflects, you know what fragile memory'll hold. Again the key falls on the flagstones. Again there are her footsteps on the road.

The last of Ireland is taken from him, its rocks, its gorse, its little harbours, the distant lighthouse. He watches until there is no land left, only the sunlight dancing over the sea.

PENGUIN ESSENTIALS

SWALLOWING GEOGRAPHY/DEBORAH LEVY

Like her namesake Jack Kerouac, J.K. is always on the road, travelling Europe with her typewriter in a pillowcase. From J.K.'s irreverent, ironic perspective, Levy charts a new, dizzying, end-of-the-century world of shifting boundaries and displaced peoples.

'An exciting writer, sharp and shocking as the knives her characters wield' *Sunday Times*

THE BASTARD OF ISTANBUL/ELIF SHAFAK

One rainy afternoon in Istanbul, a nineteen-year-old, unmarried woman walks into a doctor's surgery. 'I need to have an abortion,' she announces.

Twenty years later, Asya Kazanci lives with her extended family in Istanbul. All the Kazanci men die in their early forties, victims of the mysterious family curse, so it is a house of women. Among them are Asya's beautiful, rebellious mother, her clairvoyant aunt, and their hopelessly hypochondriac sister. Into the midst for this madhouse comes Asya's feisty American cousin, and she's bringing long-hidden family secrets connected with Turkey's turbulent past in her wake. . .

'A beautiful book, the finest I've read' *Irish Times*

ANCIENT LIGHT/JOHN BANVILLE

'*Billie Gray was my best friend and I fell in love with his mother*'

In a small Irish town a fifteen-year-old boy secretly meets a thirty-five-year-old woman. She obsesses and torments him as only a first love can. Fifty years later, Alexander Cleave - an actor grieving for the recent loss of his daughter - recalls this affair, trying to make sense of who he was, of the older woman he fell for, the friendship he betrayed and of how time and life change our sense of ourselves.

'Brilliant' *Guardian*

SUBMARINE/JOE DUNTHORNE

'*Are we making a bomb?*'

'*This is a trust exercise, like in drama,*' she says.

'*Are we making a bomb as a trust exercise?*'

Fifteen-year-old Oliver Tate is terrified that his family is falling apart. He fears for his depressed father and is convinced that his mother is having an affair with her capoeira teacher. Deciding that it is down to him alone to save his parents' marriage, Oliver sets out on a campaign to rescue it while also embarking on an even more ambitious goal: to lose his virginity before he's sixteen to the seductive but slightly pyromaniacal Jordana . . .

'The sharpest, funniest, rudest account of a troubled teenager's coming of age since *The Catcher in the Rye*' *Independent*

PENGUIN ESSENTIALS

THE ROTTERS' CLUB/JONATHAN COE

'Sometimes I feel that I am destined always to be offstage whenever the main action occurs. That God has made me the victim of some cosmic practical joke, by assigning me little more than a walk-on part in my own life . . .'

Coming of age in 1970s' Birmingham, teenager Benjamin Trotter is about to discover the agonies and ecstasies of growing up. Whether it is first love or last rites, IRA bombs or industrial strife, prog versus punk rock, expectations of bad poetry or an unexpected life-changing experience involving lost swimming trunks, *The Rotters' Club* is a heartfelt and hilarious portrait of a particular time and place featuring characters recognizable the world over . . .

'Very funny, a compulsive and gripping read' *The Times*

THE PHOTOGRAPH/PENELOPE LIVELY

'DO NOT OPEN - DESTROY.'

The words on the envelope he has found are written in Kath's hand, but Glyn ignores his wife's instruction and breaks the seal. His life unwinds. For he finds a photograph showing Kath holding hands with another man. Unable to forget this long-ago act of betrayal he recklessly excavates the past, seeking out who knew what, tearing apart other lives as he tries to dig up the roots of his wife's infidelity. But what is the truth about Kath? What is the truth about their love? And can it survive this?

'Remarkable' *Sunday Telegraph*

PENGUIN ESSENTIALS

LIFE CLASS/PAT BARKER

'*You were not allowed to talk in the life class . . .*'

It is spring, 1914, and Paul Tarrant and Elinor Brooke are students at the Slade School of Art, gathering for life-drawing classes under the tutelage of Henry Tonks. Each finds this select new world difficult and they seek solace in one another. Yet just as they are beginning to admit their feelings towards each other war breaks out and Paul joins the Belgian Red Cross. At Ypres he experiences devastation so extraordinary that he wonders if he can ever convey it to another soul . . .

'Triumphant, shattering, inspiring' *The Times*

BEAUTIFUL RUINS/JESS WALTER

'*The actress arrived in his village the only way one could come directly . . .*'

In spring 1962 American actress Dee Moray's boat motors into an Italian bay and the life of hotelier Pasquale Tursi. Dee - fleeing a film set, claiming to be dying and desperately awaiting her lover - throws herself on Pasquale's generous mercy. Fifty years later Pasquale lands in Hollywood, sporting a fedora and seeking a long-forgotten actress. Why he's come, what happened to Dee in Italy and, later, in LA, are questions that *Beautiful Ruins* answers in the most surprising and wonderfully entertaining manner.

'Exhilarating. Very, very funny' *The Times*

PENGUIN ESSENTIALS

A SPELL OF WINTER/HELEN DUNMORE

'I wanted us to wake to a kingdom of ice where our breath would turn to icicles as it left our lips, and we would walk through tunnels of snow to the outhouses and find birds fallen dead from the air . . .'

In the years just before the First World War, Cathy and her brother Rob find themselves living alone in a decaying English mansion with their distant, stern grandfather. Abandoned by their mother while their distraught father is confined to an asylum, they roam the grounds freely with little understanding of trespass. Lost in their own private world, they seek and find new lines to cross. But they are not so separate from the outside, nor as alone, as they believe . . .

'Written so seductively that passages sing out from the page'
Sunday Times

THE CASE-BOOK OF SHERLOCK HOLMES/ARTHUR CONAN DOYLE

'Come at once if convenient - if inconvenient come all the same . . .'

The note from Sherlock Holmes to Dr Watson cannot be ignored and soon the pair find themselves investigating the curious case of an aged professor, whose sudden strange alteration in behaviour terrifies everyone, from his daughter and her fiancé to the family dog. This and eleven other cases which confound clients or perplex the police are tackled by Holmes and Watson in the final collection of the duo's detecting adventures.

'Time and time again generations have shown that they need Holmes' Stephen Fry

He just wanted a decent book to read ...

Not too much to ask, is it? It was in 1935 when Allen Lane, Managing Director of Bodley Head Publishers, stood on a platform at Exeter railway station looking for something good to read on his journey back to London. His choice was limited to popular magazines and poor-quality paperbacks – the same choice faced every day by the vast majority of readers, few of whom could afford hardbacks. Lane's disappointment and subsequent anger at the range of books generally available led him to found a company – and change the world.

'We believed in the existence in this country of a vast reading public for intelligent books at a low price, and staked everything on it'
Sir Allen Lane, 1902–1970, founder of Penguin Books

The quality paperback had arrived – and not just in bookshops. Lane was adamant that his Penguins should appear in chain stores and tobacconists, and should cost no more than a packet of cigarettes.

Reading habits (and cigarette prices) have changed since 1935, but Penguin still believes in publishing the best books for everybody to enjoy. We still believe that good design costs no more than bad design, and we still believe that quality books published passionately and responsibly make the world a better place.

So wherever you see the little bird – whether it's on a piece of prize-winning literary fiction or a celebrity autobiography, political tour de force or historical masterpiece, a serial-killer thriller, reference book, world classic or a piece of pure escapism – you can bet that it represents the very best that the genre has to offer.

Whatever you like to read – trust Penguin.